ARTIFACT OF THE TRUE PATRIOT

THE DANIEL CODEX™ BOOK THREE

JUDITH BERENS   MARTHA CARR   MICHAEL ANDERLE

ARTIFACT OF THE TRUE PATRIOT TEAM

Thanks to Early Readers

Debi Sateren, Michael Robbins, Kathleen Fettig,
Terry Hicks Bennett, Bep Hvilsted-Koopman

Thanks to the JIT Readers

James Caplan
Kelly O'Donnell
Misty Roa
Mary Morris
Angel LaVey
John Ashmore
Danika Fedeli
Paul Westman
Larry Omans

If we've missed anyone, please let us know!

Editor Lynne Stiegler

From Martha

To everyone who still believes in magic
and all the possibilities that holds.
To all the readers who make this
entire ride so much fun.
And to my son, Louie and so many wonderful friends who
remind me all the time of what
really matters and how wonderful
life can be in any given moment.

From Michael

To Family, Friends and
Those Who Love
To Read.
May We All Enjoy Grace
To Live The Life We Are
Called.

CHAPTER ONE

Daniel Winters jerked his head to the side at the last second to avoid John Rainer's fist. He scrambled back with his fists up. "I underestimated you. Maybe I shouldn't have asked you to spar with me. I always thought us modern agents had better combat training, old man."

His blonde opponent grinned playfully, his blue eyes filled with mischief. "Back in my day, we didn't have a bunch of gizmos and doodads to get us out of trouble." He followed up with a series of quick jabs. "Wits and fists, that's what makes a real agent, Danny boy."

The younger man blocked the blows and threw a wide hook, but John danced out of range. Mr. Greatest Generation might be old-fashioned, but he still had good moves. He'd have made excellent backup a century before, and once they brought him up to speed, he'd be a solid asset in modern times.

The small workout area wasn't nearly as impressive as what the Company provided. It consisted only of a sparring mat on one side and weight and cardio machines on the other, but the room held enough equipment for anyone to get a full workout without ever leaving the building.

Daniel might live a double life, but not every member of their little rogue group in the brownstone did, including a few people like John and Ronni who had nowhere else to go.

The CIA agent now sparred with "the man out of time" to work off some nervous energy. The barrage of revelations in recent days had left him off-balance. Every secret peeled back a new layer of hidden truth that made him question everyone he knew. At least now, he was on the same page as his grandfather, and that meant something. They could rebuild their mutual trust, but Daniel didn't believe the world was done surprising him.

John threw another punch and almost nailed his distracted partner. "You're too slow. Do you need a gadget or two for help?"

"I'm only slow because I didn't get my coffee from Tommy today," Daniel retorted. "Otherwise, I wouldn't let an old man beat me."

John laughed. "Keep telling stories. If that makes you feel better after you go down, that's fine by me. Maybe I should complain about being dead for a while."

"Excuses, excuses." He chuckled and threw a quick jab, but the other man blocked it.

Daniel had headed out early that morning and missed his coffee because he wanted a good workout before heading to the Company. Tommy would be more than happy to take the money he'd left on the counter beside a note explaining the situation.

He spun and threw an elbow. John barely blocked it and

stumbled back. The shot had come close to finishing the match.

"No gentlemen's rules," Daniel taunted with a grin on his face. "It's all mixed martial arts these days with normal humans. Magicals add more interesting possibilities."

John snorted. "Call it what you want. I can still kick ass with the best of them. Sure, some magical dame might show up and turn me into a frog, but if it's only about shooting or punching, I can do that." He charged without warning.

"Daniel," a soft female voice called.

He turned instinctively, a costly mistake. John landed a solid punch to the side of his head, and Daniel crashed to the mat with a grunt. His head throbbed.

Ronni threw her hands over her mouth and gasped. "Are you all right?"

The older operative grunted and bounced a few times on the balls of his feet. "Sorry, Danny boy. I was already moving before she spoke. I wasn't going for a cheap shot."

Daniel pushed off the ground and shook his head to clear the pain. He rubbed it and hissed. "Like I said. No gentleman's rules, so there's nothing to apologize for. In a real fight, I can't expect no distractions." He wiped his hands on his exercise shorts and turned toward Ronni as he continued to rub the side of his head. "What's up?"

She sighed. "Paul sent me a message through my brownstone phone because he couldn't get hold of you."

"I've been busy letting John beat me up." Daniel wandered to a nearby bench, grabbed his towel, and wiped the sweat from his face and neck. "Did Paul find something?"

"He's located a few of the escaped prisoners. Not suspected aliens but, you know, regular bad guys." Ronni shrugged. "He figured you might want to go after some of them, sir."

Daniel grinned. "Regular bad guys as in dangerous magicals?"

John chuckled and shook his head.

She nibbled on her lip. "Well, they're regular compared to aliens. From what I can tell, though, they're not super-tough. Low-hanging fruit for the most part so should be easy to grab."

"Again, easy is a relative term."

Her cheek's colored. "You know what I mean. They won't blow up a building when you go after them."

John chuckled and waved. "I'll hit the showers. Nice fight, Daniel."

"Same, John." Daniel nodded to him and turned to Ronni. "Okay, send the information to my Company phone since this will technically be a company mission. Maybe capturing some of these bastards will make people less suspicious of me." He finished toweling off. "John's got the right idea. It's time to shower and get to work."

***

The agent adjusted his tie as he walked through the operations room. The holographic globe hovering over the main table dominated the center of the room, and as always, potential alien hotspots all over the world were marked in red. The more his team probed, the more leads they found. It was only a matter of staying ahead of Fortis.

He could have taken the elevator from the gym directly to the lobby, but he liked the operations room. Maybe one day, there'd be a flashing alert that Ronni or Paul had set up to warn him of an imminent alien invasion.

Imminent? Aren't they already here?

He stopped at the sight of Jake drawing at the operations table. Seeing a young boy in the middle of a secret rogue CIA operation base for alien investigation still made Daniel's stomach knot. The aliens had stolen the boy from his parents, and the kid still had no memory of his previous life. Daniel's grandfather believed some aliens were good and some were bad. The kind that stole a child's life was likely the latter sort. He couldn't think of a useful tactical or strategic reason to kidnap a young boy.

The operative walked to the table and looked at the drawing. It seemed to be a rendering of the operations room, though Jake wouldn't win art awards anytime soon.

The boy looked up and smiled. "Where are you going?"

"Paul told me about some bad guys, so I have to check in at my other job. They want me to find them."

Jake sighed. "Why don't you live here? There are beds and stuff here."

Daniel shrugged. "I'm sorry, Jake. There are people who aren't part of this group who are important to me, and I need to spend time with them, too." He tousled the kid's hair. "I understand. This isn't a home. It's a base, but we're working on a better solution for you. We'll find one. I promise you."

The boy sighed and nodded, a glum expression on his face.

The agent patted his head one more time and headed for the elevator.

Maybe the aliens don't know what they're doing, but it doesn't matter. I've got to stop them from yanking people out of their lives.

Daniel smiled as he approached the guard at the CIA building security checkpoint. He was early enough that there wasn't a line, always a bonus.

"Please lean forward, sir," the man asked, looking more bored than usual.

It was the same routine as on any other day. The agent stuck his eye against the retinal scanner.

The guard's computer beeped and he glanced at it, a slight frown on his face. All the boredom vanished off his face.

"Badge." He held out a hand; the other hovered near his gun.

Daniel maintained his smile. Maybe the man was trying to spice up a monotonous daily routine. His stomach tightened at other possibilities.

Fortis won't have a security guard kill me at a checkpoint. That would raise too many questions.

The official waved a scanner over the badge and entered some commands into the computer before moving the device over the ID again. He frowned deeper this time and sighed.

Daniel waited for the guard to hand his badge back, but he didn't. The possibility that he might have to take a guard out in the front of CIA headquarters crystallized into reality.

The security officer looked up and shook his head. "Access denied, sir. I'm afraid you'll have to wait here. You need to go to Internal Affairs, and agents will be here shortly to escort you there." He rested his hand on his gun. "Please don't try to run, sir."

"What's this about?" he asked.

"Please wait for the IA agents."

"Ah, just what I needed this morning—an IA enema."

The guard merely stared at him without even an attempt at a smile.

Daniel shrugged, folded his arms, and moved aside. The least the guy could do was give him a pity chuckle.

Less than a minute later, two dark-suited agents stepped out of the elevator on the other side of the checkpoint. They approached him from either side.

"Hand your firearm over slowly," one of them commanded.

Daniel resisted the urge to roll his eyes and complied with the instruction. The minute he had the weapon clear of his jacket, the man snatched it from his hand.

"Come with us. Sudden movements will be considered hostile." The second agent nodded toward the elevator.

"They must love you at parties," Daniel quipped. "You're a real fun guy."

The IA man grunted and shoved him through the checkpoint and toward the elevator. The other flanked his other side.

Daniel's heart rate kicked up. Executing him in the

elevator would be easier to explain away, especially if they altered or erased the camera footage.

"I don't suppose anyone will tell me what this is about?" he asked.

They ignored him.

He kept a smile plastered on his face as they entered and turned before the doors closed. Now, they wouldn't be able to surprise him. They'd need a lot more than two agents to take him out.

The trip didn't involve any threats or ambushes, merely men who glared at him in belligerent silence. His jokes might have landed with a pitiful thud, but at least no one pulled a gun on him. Any joke he could walk away from was a winner.

A trip down the mazelike hallways brought him to an interrogation room with a simple bolted-down black metal desk and a few secured chairs. Of course, they wouldn't risk a prisoner beating an agent to death with a chair. It was an annoying and embarrassing way to die in CIA headquarters.

Knowing the procedure, Daniel sat on the opposite side of the table and folded his arms. The agents had disarmed him, but they'd left everything else, including his phones. He wasn't sure if that increased or decreased the chance that he would be assassinated, though he suspected they had jammed the room.

After five minutes, a dark-haired man with a weathered face entered with a tablet in hand. He sat across from Daniel. "Agent Winters."

Daniel nodded. "Last time I checked. And you are?"

"Special Agent Tomlinson. Internal Affairs." He folded

his hands in front of him. "Is there anything you want to say before we get this started?"

Daniel grinned. "I hear the Nationals might go all the way this year. Forget Oriceran, that's the real magic."

Tomlinson blinked but didn't frown or crack a smile.

He must practice that expression in a mirror.

"That's your only statement?" the man asked.

"Yes." Daniel shrugged. "Wait. That, and well, politicians suck, but maybe that's why they built D.C. on top of a stinking swamp."

"Real funny guy, huh?"

"That's what my friends tell me."

"I'm not your friend." Tomlinson tapped on the tablet and spun it so Daniel could see a half-dozen mugshots on the screen. He swiped and brought up another six, then again for even more portraits of the world's deadliest prisoners.

Daniel recognized them all if only because he'd seen several CIA reports and bulletins on them in recent days. They were all escapees from the hidden ultramax in CIA headquarters, but not from Hangar Twelve.

Relief spread through him. Whatever this was about, it didn't seem to involve aliens, which made it less likely that Fortis was pulling the strings.

"A nice collection of scum bags," Daniel commented. He pointed at a couple of them. "Not as tough as Saram, though. They'll go down pretty damned easily." He shrugged.

Tomlinson leaned back. "To be clear, your security clearance has temporarily been revoked in connection with the mass breakout."

Daniel forced a playful snort. If he treated the accusations as ridiculous, he'd have a better chance to talk his way out of the situation. If they already had direct evidence he was involved, they wouldn't bother with the tight-lipped interrogation tactics. The ironic thing was if the CIA brass weren't so afraid of magic, they could use artifacts or spells to make such interrogations far more efficient.

They're always fighting the last war.

"So, what? I helped a bunch of scum escape, and then I go and almost get myself killed hunting them down?" Daniel shook his head. "That's not my style, and I have better things to do."

Tomlinson's expression remained unchanged—flat and disinterested. "Where were you during the incident?"

"On my way home. I left about twenty minutes before it started."

"And can you prove you were on your way home?" Tomlinson blinked yet again, perhaps the only sign he was a human.

Daniel shrugged. "I'm sure if you cross-check the exit logs and the tracking on my phone, they will confirm my story."

He spoke with confidence. Paul and Ronni had insured they would and had inserted fake footage of him in case the CIA went digging into traffic cameras or drone recordings. Agents had seen him during the chaos, but the helpful chameleon mask ensured they didn't recognize him. He also knew IA would already have checked on that.

They have crap. This is simple fishing. They're probably asking everyone who left around that time.

Tomlinson stood. He clasped his hands behind his back and paced methodically. "Pretty convenient, don't you think? Leaving shortly before one of the worst mass escapes in Company history?"

Daniel shrugged. "Coincidence is real, and I'm not the idiot who thought hiding an ultramax in the headquarters basement was a great idea. I've done what every agent with free time has done—looked for these guys and brought them in or taken them out."

The IA agent stopped and stared at him. "A few sacrifices, Mr. Winters, would be useful if you wanted to cover up the escapes of others."

"Sure, but that doesn't make it true." Daniel pointed at the tablet and uttered one of the few sentences that would be completely true even if they'd used magic to test him. "I didn't knowingly try and help any of those ultramax assholes escape." He held the man's stare. "I wasn't even in the building. Like I said, check my phone records and the exit logs. I don't know what else to tell you."

Tomlinson sat again and grabbed the tablet. He tapped a few times, the sound loud above the faint whir of the air passing through vents overhead. The typing continued for several minutes before he set the device down.

"You're excused, Agent Winters," he muttered without looking up. "My men will reissue your firearm. Your clearance has been restored."

Daniel frowned as he stood. "So you dragged me in here to screw with me?"

Tomlinson responded with a bland look. "The internal security of the CIA is paramount." He motioned toward the door. "I don't apologize for doing my job."

One of the other agents already stood at the door with Daniel's gun.

He took the weapon and holstered it. "Are you questioning everybody?"

"Have a good day, Agent Winters."

Daniel shrugged and headed toward the closest elevator.

He might have been fishing, but if I hadn't covered my ass so well, I would have been screwed. That was close. Too damned close.

Paul had sent information on some of the missing prisoners through normal channels, and Daniel was eager to hit the streets and clean his mess up. He'd already had a discussion with the hacker about planning things a little more carefully, and Paul seemed to realize his error with the breakout—or, at least, he pretended to. Daniel was done underestimating the other man because of his quirks.

"Let's see," the agent murmured under his breath. "Whose ass do I want to kick today? There are so many choices. It's almost like a game."

A shadow fell over him, and someone cleared her throat delicately behind him.

He turned in his chair to see an attractive young woman holding a tablet. She was dressed professionally—blue skirt, white shirt, and flats—but the outfit didn't really scream agent. Her cool blue eyes surveyed him from beneath her light eyebrows. She pursed her lips and looked him up and down.

Daniel stared at her for a moment, waiting for her to speak. She seemed vaguely familiar, but he couldn't place her.

"I'm Lucy," she declared finally.

He nodded slowly. "Agent Daniel Winters. Is there something I can help you with?"

Lucy looked at the tablet and tapped in a few commands. His phone chimed a few seconds later.

"I've sent you briefing information on your next mission." She nodded curtly.

Daniel frowned. "I was about to follow up on capturing some of the escaped prisoners."

"They can wait, or another agent can handle them." Her gaze cut to his screen with a look of disapproval, as if she expected to see porn instead of files on dangerous magicals. "Oh, I suppose I should explain who I am."

"It might be helpful, yeah."

"I'm your new dedicated support." Lucy lifted her chin, a certain arrogance to the gesture. "I'll be honest, Agent Winters. I think more than a few people don't trust you since you worked so closely with that traitor Welch, but I volunteered to help with some of her previous responsibilities. I think it's unfair to blame you for that woman's deception."

"How magnanimous of you." Daniel held back his smile, even though he wanted to share a few choice words about insulting Ronni.

She nodded but didn't smile. He began to wonder if she was capable of it.

"Your last name isn't Tomlinson, is it?" he asked.

Lucy frowned and shook her head. "No. Greenville. Why?"

He shrugged. "No reason. You remind me of someone I recently talked to."

Daniel resisted a smirk. There could easily be more than one person in CIA with an allergy to smiling. Maybe he could find an artifact to help those sad, poor, unhappy souls.

Lucy scowled with faint disapproval. She tapped the tablet. "Paraguay, Agent Winters. This is a time-sensitive mission. There's a new type of Oriceran artifact there the agency needs recovered from a group of independent researchers. Not terrorists, per se, but they have flagrantly violated several international laws, which is why they're hiding in rural Paraguay."

The agent shrugged. "Sounds simple enough."

"Perhaps. This is a type of implant. Biomagical technology." Her voice dripped with contempt.

Daniel wasn't fond of the idea himself. The Company had run into that combination on and off through the last few decades, and it rarely ended well. Everyone was convinced they could make someone live longer, be stronger, or cure a disease, but there was still a long way to go when it came to mixing technology and magic safely in living things.

Too many people wanted to play God with technology, and adding magic to the mix only made things worse. Most governments on Earth and Oriceran, along with the UN and other transnational bodies, had passed extensive laws and regulations against it. The strictures didn't stop people from trying, obviously.

Daniel sighed and shook his head. "Implant? So, it's already in someone?"

"Something." Lucy shrugged. "A cow. A prototype, I suppose. Allegedly, this particular implant leaves subjects alive even after they have suffered severe damage that would otherwise be lethal." Her face twitched. "They've hurt that poor animal. The test subject will, unfortunately, have to be killed to recover the implant, which should be in the brain according to our information."

Daniel nodded. "That's tough, but it's more merciful than keeping it alive. It's too bad they wasted a perfectly good pile of hamburgers."

She snorted her disgust. "I'm a vegan. All the relevant information has been transferred to your Company phone. Contact me when you're in-country if you need anything, but I fail to see why this should require active support. If you think you do need it, let me know, and I'll arrange things appropriately. You'll also find an equipment list in your background documents. Everything will be prepared by the time you're ready to leave."

"You want me to go after a dangerous artifact, but you won't have my back directly?" Daniel arched a brow.

She didn't turn to face him. "Field agents shouldn't need their hands held. You can put a formal request in if you have an issue with that."

Lucy walked away, and Daniel stared after her.

Talk about the anti-Ronni.

CHAPTER TWO

The rental truck rattled alarmingly as Daniel sped down the cracked and weather-worn road leading to the coordinates. The lab was located near a small town in the foothills of a local mountain. According to his briefing documents, they received enough tourist traffic that some random gringo in a fancy gray rental truck shouldn't raise an immediate eyebrow.

His Codex phone rang with a call from Timothy, and he answered it on speakerphone.

"What's up, Tim?"

His mentor cleared his throat. "I've poked around quietly and asked about the IA interrogation."

Daniel snorted. "Yeah, that was fun, although I don't know who is more annoying, Troy Williams or Special Agent Tomlinson. Is Tomlinson on your list of possible Fortis agents?"

Timothy sighed. "No, not at all. That's what worries me. It means if they do suspect you, they'll play this smart, like they did with Ronni. They'll burn you, then assassinate you."

"It's not like I imagined they'd challenge me to a Jenga match, winner take all." Daniel checked his mirrors, then his rearview camera. No one was following him. "Besides, it's logical that they questioned me because of the apparent timing of my exit."

"No," the older agent replied. Daniel could hear his stress ball squeaking over the line. "That's just it. I thought that at first too, but you're one of the few who were questioned. You're right to some degree, though. It was all agents who'd left shortly before the break-in. The Company's extremely spooked about this. It's bad enough that prisoners got away, but they don't know exactly how or who helped them."

"We hadn't planned to help them." He eased the accelerator down a little. No traffic meant less risk of an accident. "Paul's help was both impressive and terrible at the same time. Terribly impressive?"

Tim snorted. "I'm still not sure about him. He's too unpredictable for my tastes and far too convinced of his own self-righteousness."

Daniel barked out a laugh. "And we aren't? He's agreed to plan better in the future. That's all we can ask. At least with the abductees returned, we're a little closer to more information. The Company's locating the escaped prisoners one by one, so I'm not too worried about them."

"True enough, but take care, Daniel. I've got to go. I need to head over to the Company soon for another meeting about the breakout. Be careful down there."

"I always am."

Tim ended the call.

Maybe it's a pipe dream, but it'd be nice if, at some point in the future, I didn't have to lie to the CIA. There are simply too many damned lies.

Daniel frowned. Tim had held information back from him before. His grandfather might have come clean, but his mentor hadn't, and that was an itch Daniel would need to scratch soon. There were only so many secret agendas he could handle.

For the moment, he had a nice straight-forward mission—if capturing a biomagical implant was considered normal.

The town appeared on the horizon—not huge, but not a village either. That made sense. It wasn't feasible to hide a strange research facility near a tiny settlement where everyone knew everyone else. Daniel didn't know the exact location, but his regional contact insisted he already had the information but wouldn't reveal the site's locale without meeting him face-to-face.

Maybe I should look at some of the ranches on the edge of town for clues first.

He slowed as he approached some fenced-off pasture-land. A half-dozen cows munched lazily and ignored the vehicle. He stopped the truck and stepped out.

In the distance, a muscular old man wearing a straw hat watched him for a few seconds before he rushed toward a nearby house with surprising speed.

"Okay," the agent murmured. "I wonder what that was

about. Maybe I should have checked in with my contact first."

It wasn't like he was an expert on Paraguay, even if he could speak decent Spanish. Foreign travelers always ran the risk of causing offense.

Daniel wandered a little way down the road and studied the cows. They all appeared normal enough. His furtive examination revealed several fenced-off pastures, most with a handful of animals. The locals stuck to small-scale production, which was consistent with what his briefing indicated.

A minute had passed when he noticed movement around the house. Eight men and two women rushed toward him. Normally, he wouldn't worry about a group of random farmers, but these were armed. Most brandished machetes or pitchforks, and two men who didn't carried large kitchen knives that glinted in the sun.

"I guess I should be happy they don't have guns, but I know a murderous mob when I see one," he muttered.

Daniel turned toward his truck. The group didn't seem to be in the mood to talk.

They closed on him, and he picked up the pace.

"*Ladrón de ganado!*" one of the men screamed. "*Gringo ladrón.*" He flourished a machete with unmistakable vehemence.

Okay, so some other gringos have shown up and stolen cattle. It sounds like I'm in the right place at least.

Daniel broke into a sprint. He could easily gun them down, but murdering a group of farmers who were angry about losing valuable property to foreign thieves wasn't why he'd joined the CIA. They were likely also victims of the twisted assholes testing their life implants on random, unsuspecting cows.

The shouts drew closer, but the mob couldn't match the agent's speed. He threw the door of his truck open, hopped inside, and started the engine. The vehicle roared and sped down the road. He jerked the wheel to the side to avoid the mob, but they did get sprayed with dust and dirt for their efforts.

He stared into the rearview camera display for a wide-angle view. The farmers gestured angrily with their weapons, but they didn't follow him or rush toward their houses or any vehicles.

"Great," Daniel mumbled. "Lucy's background information didn't mention any of that."

A trip across town increased the distance from the anti-rustler mob and brought him to a rickety, one-story wooden building that was theoretically a bar. The ramshackle structure and rotting wood suggested an experiment in how many people could walk in and out of a trap before it collapsed and killed them.

Daniel stepped out of the truck and glanced over his shoulder. The farmers hadn't somehow teleported across town, and only a few older women frowned at him.

Do they think I'm going in there to score?

He tried a friendly grin. They scoffed and hurried away but continued to whisper amongst themselves and point at him.

Daniel turned toward the bar. A sad neon sign reading

EL INFIERNO hung over the entrance. Only half the letters were lit, and several others flickered. So much for it being hell. Even the doorknob looked ready to fall.

He pulled the door open and wrinkled his nose at the overwhelming acrid and fruity scent. A half-dozen lowlifes sat inside the darkened establishment, most sipping drinks at the bar. A few others slumped over their tables. A slow and mournful Guarani ballad about lost love played at a low volume.

A quick look around netted Daniel his contact in the corner, a smiling brown-skinned man in a gray-and-black wool poncho typical of the area. Despite the many wrinkles in his face, he didn't look nearly as old as Daniel knew he was.

The agent's shoes splashed through a few shallow pools of water. His wizard contact couldn't have picked a seedier place if he'd tried.

He sat at the table with a frown. "Nice place, Miguel. I love how no matter what country I'm in, I end up in places like this. A tour of the underbelly of the world."

Miguel chuckled quietly. "When you do things that you don't want people to know about, this is the right kind of place." He spoke English with only the faintest accent, and it was more Castilian than local. He nodded at a man a few tables down who was passed-out drunk. "This is a place where people come to forget the outside world, my friend."

Daniel shrugged. "I could do with some of that after stopping at the ranches on the edge of town."

Miguel winced. "Bad idea." A smile followed. "But you're still alive, so no problem, right?"

"Yeah, I figured out it was a bad idea once the armed mob came after me."

The man shrugged, and the motion moved his poncho a little to reveal a wand holster. "You can't blame them. This is a poor rural area. A single cow is much of their wealth."

"I don't blame them." Daniel retrieved his silence cube from his pocket. He activated it, set it on the table, and the light chatter and music faded. "I blame whoever is experimenting on cows with biomagical implants."

Miguel nodded slowly and leaned forward. "I know where the lab is. It's close. They took over an old abandoned military warehouse not too far from town." He nodded toward the bar. "Locals won't go near it. We hear bad rumors about that place to begin with. It closed after a few murders during some black-market smuggling deal, and now, people are convinced there are ghosts. They're scared they will disappear if they go there."

Daniel frowned. "There aren't, are there? Ghosts?"

The old wizard shook his head. "Magic is there, but no ghosts. I haven't gotten too close. I didn't want to make whoever was inside nervous. People have disappeared, but it's not ghosts that are responsible. It's gringo wizards and scientists." He muttered a curse in Spanish. "Do you know how long I've lived in Paraguay?"

"No."

"Over a hundred years." Miguel shook his head. "Most of the magical trouble has happened in the big cities or places like old Jesuit ruins. These small towns tend to be ignored, even after all the big magic came back." He took a deep breath. "Not that getting paid by people like you isn't nice, my friend."

Daniel moved his foot into a small puddle. He grimaced and shifted position, not sure the fluid was water. "I'm not only paying you for information. I'm paying you to come with me."

Miguel nodded. "Don't worry. I'll have your back until you're dead. Then, I'll run away. I hope you didn't think I'd avenge you."

"I'll be dead. I won't care much either way."

"You want something to eat? It'll be a long day. They have nice *chipa* here."

The agent surveyed the dark hole again—every puddle and strange stain, and the furtive small-creature movements in the shadows under tables. "Nah, I'm good. I got a Larabar left from the airport."

<hr>

Daniel donned his gear and activated the zoom on his AR glasses. He'd parked a good quarter-mile from the location. There were no obvious vehicles or drones, and from the outside, it looked like an abandoned warehouse. Weeds had long since infiltrated the cement around the building.

A few collapsed signs might have said something about not trespassing, but they were mostly rusted metal with bare hints of color under the dust, rocks, and weeds.

"You don't know what you're getting into, my friend," Miguel murmured. "This could be very dangerous."

The agent grinned. "That's part of the fun. Keep in mind that you don't get the rest of the payment if you don't come with me."

His companion waved a hand. "I know, but I'm telling you to be careful."

"I could run a drone."

The wizard scoffed. "Why don't you shoot off a flare?"

"Yeah, good point. Invisibility it is." He withdrew a chameleon ball from his tactical belt. "I didn't notice any bullet-riddled cars or charred wrecks."

Miguel frowned. "Huh?"

Daniel opened the door, stepped out, and gestured toward the warehouse. "Give me about five minutes, then drive the truck up. You look local, so they probably won't shoot immediately."

"Probably? You crazy gringo." Miguel sighed. "Sometimes, I ask myself if I really need money that bad."

Daniel shrugged. "You're a wizard. If anything bad happens, use magic." He activated the chameleon ball and the light warped around him. The SAD might have been able to stabilize the device in recent weeks, but the optical camouflage was still imperfect. Anyone looking too closely would see his outline. It'd still be good enough to cross the mostly open terrain toward the warehouse, however.

The CIA agent kicked into a brisk jog. His gaze swept the area, looking for anything out of place. No sentries, drones, or strange glowing butterflies caused any alarm. That was a good start, at least. If the little mad scientists inside were arrogant, they might never anticipate the CIA coming after them. It'd be easy to scare locals off without putting too much effort into things.

Almost there.

He smiled as he neared the warehouse. Signs of more recent habitation began to appear, such as visibly newer repairs to the roof he hadn't noticed from a distance and weeds bent parallel to the ground. Someone had been there recently.

The hum of the truck's engine grew closer. Miguel was on the move.

Daniel approached the side of the structure, his optical camouflage still active. He frowned as he approached the door and saw the lock was shot out.

He drew his gun and rushed toward the front, staying close to the wall. The lock in the front had also been damaged. What he could see through the small dust-covered window showed an unoccupied front room, pieces of old cabinets strewn around, and piles of refuse dragged in by animals.

Something doesn't feel right.

Once Miguel arrived, the agent disabled the chameleon ball and hurried toward the idling truck.

The wizard rolled down the window. "Whatever happened to surprising them?"

Daniel checked his pistol. "My gut says they were already surprised. Back me up."

Miguel sighed and stepped out of the vehicle. He drew his thick bone wand and followed as the CIA agent crept toward the front door.

"On three, two, one." Daniel threw the door open and spun inside to sweep the first room for targets. "Shit."

A muscular man with a gun sprawled on the ground as if waiting in ambush. Daniel almost fired but stopped at the last moment and walked over to him.

Even though his eyes were open, he wasn't breathing and had a bullet hole in the middle of his forehead.

The agent holstered his pistol. "Cover me for a moment."

Miguel grunted and raised his wand.

Daniel pulled some thin gloves on and felt the man's neck. "There's no pulse, but he's still warm. The color is good in his face, too, so he died recently." He readied his weapon again and walked toward the hallway. After a silent three-count using his fingers, he spun around the corner.

A couple more bodies littered the hallway. Given their builds, one was a guard or hired muscle. A wiry corpse with glasses and no weapon was likely a researcher. Both had been shot.

The agent jogged down the hallway to the main warehouse floor and grabbed a flashbang. He flattened himself against the wall. The door was open with yet another guard's body in front of it.

"Wait for me, my friend," Miguel called.

Instead, Daniel threw the flashbang. After the pop of the explosion, he rushed inside, his pistol ready. He found more bodies, including several in lab jackets and a couple of corpses clutching wands.

A dead cow lay inside a metal enclosure, the top of its skull removed to expose its brain. Multiple gunshot wounds marred the animal's bulk. Several cuts into its side had been clamped open. The edges of the head wound were jagged as if someone had worked in a hurry.

Daniel frowned. There wasn't as much blood as he would have expected. If the animal was already dead before its head was opened, that might explain it.

"*Dios mío*," Miguel muttered. He raised his wand and

uttered an incantation in Spanish. A few seconds later, a bright wave of energy blasted from his wand. It swept over the agent and left a lingering warmth.

"What was that?" He looked at the wizard with an eyebrow raised.

Miguel held up a finger and didn't speak for several seconds. "I'm checking to see if there was anyone or anything left alive. I didn't do it before because I didn't want to alert any wizards, but everyone here looks like they were shot."

"And?"

The old man shook his head. "Nothing but death here."

Daniel holstered his gun and walked closer to the cow. "I guess my briefing was right. The implant must have been in the brain." He nodded toward the door. "Someone beat us to the punch, but it couldn't have been all that long ago. Maybe even minutes."

Miguel frowned. "But we didn't see anyone on the way here. Wouldn't they have had to pass us? If they went overland, wouldn't we have seen the dust cloud?"

"Not if they came from the opposite direction on the road." Daniel grinned and jogged to the door. "Time for a good old-fashioned chase."

CHAPTER THREE

Miguel maintained a white-knuckled death grip on the door as the vehicle barreled down the road and shook noisily. The agent had driven to the town north of Asunción, but more than a few cities with airports lay in the opposite direction. He assumed that whoever had attacked the warehouse weren't locals, although a drug lord could find a good use for the implant.

He frowned. That didn't make sense. A drug lord would have taken the researchers, too. Killing everybody indiscriminately meant they'd cut themselves off from potentially useful research.

Several minutes had passed when Daniel saw the black SUV in the distance. They traveled fast but not at the same cracking pace as him. He closed quickly on the vehicle and changed lanes a few hundred feet before he reached them. Maybe he could avoid an immediate attack if he lulled their suspicions.

Miguel sucked in a sharp breath. "Do you actually have a plan, my friend?"

The agent grinned. "Step one: find the guys who took the implant. Step two: get the implant. Step three: take the implant back to the US."

"Such a wonderful plan. So intricate in detail."

"Isn't it, though?" Daniel eased up on the gas with the SUV now only about a hundred feet away. The other vehicle hadn't taken evasive maneuvers or speeded up, which could be encouraging or a prelude to hostilities.

He grabbed his Company phone and dialed Lucy. It was time for her to do something useful.

She answered after the third ring. "Did you need something, Agent Winters?"

Daniel slowed a little to allow a distance of a few car lengths between him and the SUV. They still hadn't altered speed.

He rattled off a license plate number. "It's a long shot, but can you tell me who owns that vehicle?"

"One moment." She said nothing for a long time.

The two men continued to watch their target. If the occupants were innocent, they'd have no reason to race away.

Did I make the wrong call? Are they simply some random people?

Lucy sighed. "Is this some sort of joke?"

Daniel grunted. "I'm in the middle of Paraguay on the tail of an SUV filled with men who probably killed everybody at the lab and stole the implant. No, it's not a damned joke. Answer the question."

"You don't have to be rude." He could almost hear her frown over the line. "But I guess that explains it."

"Explains what?"

"That license plate belongs to a vehicle rented using a Company-linked account, but I don't understand why they'd be there. It's most likely Agent Lowry."

"Give me his Company mobile number."

She obliged after a few seconds of typing.

"I'll let you know how this turns out." Daniel ended the call before she could protest. The last thing he needed was another discussion, and he didn't trust her yet. He immediately dialed the number. He knew the man in passing but hadn't worked with him.

"I'm kind of busy right now," Lowry growled once he answered.

Daniel chuckled. "Yeah, busy running away from me in the truck. Pull over. We need to talk."

"I...see."

The SUV slowed, and both vehicles pulled up off the road.

Daniel nodded to his companion. "Stay in the car. If they shoot me, I'm sorry about the rest of the money."

Miguel frowned. "Who the hell is it? I don't get it."

"More Company men." The agent shrugged. "Don't get involved no matter what happens."

"That's fine by me. If you get killed, it was nice knowing you."

Daniel chuckled and glanced at the SUV. Four dark-suited agents emerged. Three, he didn't recognize, but one huge, bearded bear of a man he did. Agent Lowry.

The question remained whether any of them were Fortis agents. Shooting Daniel in CIA headquarters, either at the entrance or in the interrogation room, would leave too much evidence. Killing him on the road in rural Paraguay, not so much.

He resisted a frown. The men hadn't lain in wait for him. Something wasn't right, though, but he wasn't sure what.

Miguel kept his wand below the windshield. He chanted a spell, and his eyes glowed for a moment.

"What are you doing?" the agent asked. "Don't provoke them."

"You dragged me into your crazy gringo spy shit. I'm only making sure I can take a few bullets if they shoot me." Miguel glared at him.

"Don't worry. This should end without shooting. I think. Well, I hope."

Daniel stepped out of the truck and strolled toward the others with his hands free in case he needed his gun. He had little chance against four trained agents without cover or backup, but he didn't want to either provoke them or make things too easy for them.

He smiled and waved. "Good afternoon, gentlemen."

Lowry looked at the truck. "Who's that?" A light Southern accent colored his speech, which was consistent with what Daniel had heard from the man before.

"Local magical contractor. He was helping me track down a biomagical implant being tested on cattle. I'm assuming you and your friends have it now."

Agent Lowry nodded curtly. "We just recovered it."

Daniel still smiled, his hands close to his jacket. "I don't get it. Why would they send me if they'd already sent four other agents? Five agents for one implant is overkill. The Company's not known to get that kind of thing wrong."

I hope those aren't my last words. They aren't very epic.

The large man shrugged. "It's not like the Company never makes mistakes. We didn't mean to poach but were already coming back from something further south. Maybe someone tasked us without checking if anyone else was already on the way. Crossed wires, I guess."

Daniel nodded. "Sure, sure. But why wipe out everyone back at that lab? With your numbers, you could have at least captured the researchers."

"You know how it goes. The guards attacked, and we responded. Some of those poor sons of bitches were simply caught in the crossfire." Agent Lowry snorted. "You know the kind of shit they were working on. We did the world a favor." He waved a hand dismissively. "Anyway. We got the implant. You can go catch a matinee with your local friend there."

"We're in rural Paraguay, not D.C.," Daniel replied. "There aren't exactly a lot of theaters around. Besides, I flew a long way and almost got killed by a mob of angry farmers. I think I at least deserve a peek. Mind if I take a look?"

The other man frowned. "Actually, we do. We have a schedule, which you've already fucked up by forcing this little delay. So, if you don't mind, we'd like to get back in our vehicle and leave. Besides, we have the chain of custody to worry about."

"What the hell? Since when does the CIA care about the chain of custody for field agent collections?" Daniel narrowed his eyes.

Lowry turned to leave, and his hand dropped near his

jacket. The other men's hands lingered there as well. If he pushed too hard, he'd gain a few new holes.

I should have had Miguel cast that spell on me.

Daniel shrugged. "What a waste of time."

"Hey, think of it as a free vacation." The others turned toward their SUV, keeping an eye on Daniel.

After a quick wave, he returned to his truck. No one had shot him, but he somehow knew he'd never hear about the implant again.

He jerked the door open and slipped inside. "No one's dead. That's good."

Miguel shook his head. "No one's dead here. There are plenty of dead people at that lab."

"Good point."

The agent started the truck and turned. With a frown, he watched Lowry's SUV disappear in his rearview mirror. His instincts told him something more than simple crossed wires was involved, but he had no proof. Even though he'd attacked other agents recently, he refused to do it unless he was sure they were corrupt and way over the line. Being an asshole wasn't a capital crime.

He'd ask Tim and have Ronni ask Paul to check into things as well. If the four agents were Fortis, then it might signal that they were working to undermine Daniel. At least they'd left without too much trouble, though.

"Like I said, not knowing is half the fun." He shook his head and grinned at Miguel.

It's time to call Lucy and let her know we came up dry, but at least someone has the implant.

Daniel grumbled as he stepped onto the Metro. The mission had been a complete and utter waste of time, and his return had only proved the universe was out to get him. He'd landed late, got to his car late, parked it in the garage late, and now, he was on the last Metro back to his neighborhood.

"Yo, bro!" yelled a buzzcut twenty-something in a Georgetown shirt. He high-fived a similar-looking man. Both were red-faced and sweating.

"That party was fucking epic," the other man replied. "Chest bump!"

They collided with a loud thud. Several other passengers eyed them with distaste.

A mix of young men and women, most in their late teens and early twenties, choked the rest of the train car. Their inane, drunken chatter created a roar that made Daniel's already aching head throb more.

He rubbed his temples as he made his way further down, looking for an open seat. "Yeah, this is fucking wonderful."

His eyelids were heavy, and he wanted nothing more than to lie down and doze off with no concerns about loud college students, implants, dangerous Fortis agents, or rude support staff. The glamorous globetrotting life had more annoyances than many realized.

A sour odor assaulted his nose, and he sighed. There was only one seat left beside a woman who'd already decorated the floor with the contents of her stomach. She was passed out, her head facing the opposite way as if she didn't have the strength to lift it. Or maybe her stomach now empty, he thought belligerently.

He took the seat reluctantly.

Here's hoping.

The agent wandered down the street in his neighborhood, his hands in his pockets. It wasn't all that long ago that thugs had prowled Old Town looking for victims, but he didn't see so much as a suspicious teen or stray dog. Everything was closed, even the little corner grocery store where he'd made an example of a gang member.

He glanced above several of the stores. Most of the local owners lived over their shops. No lights were on, and everyone was content in their beds.

That's how things should be. They shouldn't worry about thugs or dangerous visitors. They shouldn't have to form mobs to chase outsiders off if people like me do our damned jobs.

A howl sounded in the distance. A shifter, he assumed— merely another aspect of living in a future no one had ever expected.

Daniel reached his own store, Rooney's Antiquities and Oddities. A soft smile formed on his face.

No strange CIA factions or no drunk college kids awaited him, only a little normal rest. Well, as normal as a man could anticipate when he slept above a shop filled with magical artifacts.

CHAPTER FOUR

He opened the door and stepped quietly into the shop. There was no reason to wake his grandfather or Tommy because he'd had an exhausting and pointless trip. He made his way into the back room to check on the half-elf.

A table had been pushed aside, making room for the boy's cot. Tommy slumbered peacefully within a sleeping bag.

He could have taken my bed upstairs. I would have been happy to hit the couch, but then again...

The agent smiled. A boy on a cot surrounded by racks of comic books—in one sense, it was a dream. It would have been Daniel's dream sleeping arrangement when he was Tommy's age, and even without the cot, it often was.

His smile faded. The kid had gone from occasionally staying over to all but living there, often eating his breakfast and taking his shower there even if he didn't sleep over. Daniel would have to address the situation sooner rather than later. The half-elf couldn't stay there forever, and why hadn't his father shown up and asked where his kid was?

Daniel shook his head. Tommy's only bruising had been from when the gang beat him. He didn't limp or show any signs of injuries. He'd insisted his father never hit him, but there was more happening than merely his father's insistence that Tommy become a musician.

I'll guess I'll have to have a chat with him soon.

He turned to leave but hesitated at the door to glance at a picture frame nearby. His father smiled in the picture, standing alone in front of the Eiffel Tower. Most of the pictures lay face down by Daniel's choice, so Tommy must have stood the picture up.

The agent stared at the photo for a moment. As busy as his parents were with their globetrotting adventures, they'd always made time for him. Both had helped make him the man he was.

A wave of nostalgia surged, and he shook his head. He wanted to believe they were alive, but that might be nothing more than wishful thinking, the dream of a teen left in the soul of a world-weary man.

"If you're alive, I'll find you," Daniel murmured.

A scratching noise and a thump sounded from the basement. Daniel narrowed his eyes and advanced to the door. He opened it, hoping it wouldn't squeak, and crept down the stairs. The basement light was already on.

He reached the bottom. The hidden vault was not only visible. It was open.

Daniel drew his gun and took a deep breath. He'd never forgotten that someone—mostly likely Fortis or someone else associated with the Company—had broken into the shop but not stolen anything. That might have been because they hadn't found what they were looking for on their first trip.

Someone murmured from inside the vault. The agent took a few quiet steps closer, his gun at the ready. He listened as someone moved around inside. A single set of footfalls sounded, and he only heard one voice.

No, he decided and holstered his pistol. Whoever it was, he needed to take them alive, either by knocking them out with a fist or with the paralysis dart in his watch. He nodded and walked toward the edge of the door.

"Damn it," the voice grumbled. He now recognized the intruder as his grandfather.

Relief flooded through Daniel, and he strolled into the vault. "What are you doing messing with the vault when Tommy's upstairs?"

Peter jumped, clearly startled by his sudden appearance. The two molecular rearrangement guns lay on a nearby shelf.

He put a hand on his chest and took a deep breath. "Are you trying to give me a heart attack?"

The agent shook his head. "I came home in the middle of the night, and I heard noises from the basement. Given everything that's happened, that's not the kind of thing I'm willing to ignore. Like I said, Tommy's upstairs."

Peter snorted. "And he's asleep. The kid could sleep through a nuclear war." He waved a hand. "And the middle of the night is the best time to do this sort of thing. There's less chance of anyone else interrupting me. Unless you think I should mess around with special hidden alien artifacts at noon."

"Fair enough." Daniel nodded at the guns. "Those things are bad news. Such bad news that you got rid of the control rod for one. Is that what you're doing this time?"

"I wouldn't do that again without telling you." His grandfather grunted and lifted his hand to reveal a notched rod. "This is the control rod from the second gun. I wanted to see if they looked the same." He gestured to the shelf. The fake control rod lay beside the other weapon.

Given that his grandfather had already told Daniel the truth about the gun he'd sabotaged, he was inclined to believe him. It helped that the old man didn't look nervous or irritated at all, only surprised.

Daniel nodded and maneuvered through the racks and tables. "Why?"

"We can hide these, but I doubt they're the only ones around." Peter shrugged. "We need to know what we're dealing with, but from what I can tell, at least with the naked eye, these look identical. I'm sure there's some difference, but this does make it seem like these things are a more standard issue and not some special custom gear handed to aliens."

His grandson took the fake control rod and turned it a few times in his hands. It was lighter than he'd expected. "One thing bothers me."

"What?"

"First, I thought this was major hardware for our visitors." Daniel set the artifact back on the shelf. "But they've been left in random places. If this is supposed to be an invasion, why do all the soldiers leave their guns lying around? It doesn't make any sense."

Peter shrugged. "Your guess is as good as mine. I don't

think it's an invasion at all, but I'm not saying there aren't some alien criminals who might be on Earth." He put his rod beside the other gun. "Maybe we should get rid of this rod."

Daniel sighed and folded his arms. "I'm not sure. It's like you said. These probably aren't the only ones around, and part of me thinks we should keep one in case we need it as a countermeasure. The aliens might not be an invasion force, but we can't be sure of that. Even if it's only a few alien criminals, I don't want some other-worldly serial killer walking around with one of these things and for us to have nothing to defend ourselves."

His grandfather nodded and slipped the rods back into place. "Then we keep it for now."

The agent stared out of the vault door, thinking about Tommy sleeping upstairs. Between the aliens, the CIA, and his domestic situation, things had only grown more complicated.

He yawned widely and rubbed the back of his neck. "You know what? I don't even want to think about this. I need to get some sleep. My mission to Paraguay was a total fucking waste of time. I'm half convinced the Company was pulling my chain."

Peter frowned and nodded. "You know, it might come down to you having to leave. You should keep that in mind."

"Maybe." Daniel shrugged. "But I can still do far more good within the CIA than I can outside of it. I'll stick with them until I have no other choice. Goodnight, Pops. I suggest you finish up here. I don't think either of us is ready to explain this to Tommy."

"Goodnight, Daniel."

He headed to the entrance to the vault. Secrets within secrets. Lies within lies. His life would be much easier if he didn't care, but that would never happen. Even the Fortis agents he'd run into before weren't sociopathic lunatics. From the little he'd heard from them, they also thought they were doing the right thing and protecting the country and the planet from an alien threat.

The weary agent shook his head and stepped out of the vault. It was like John had said a while back. Everybody always thought they were the good guy.

Maybe it's arrogance, but I'm at least a semi-good guy.

Another yawn ambushed him. He could brood tomorrow. Right now, sleep beckoned.

The next morning, after a refreshing sleep and some Killer ESP coffee, delivered courtesy of Tommy, Daniel made his way to the Company Jaguar in the private garage. He turned the car onto the street as Paul called on his Codex phone.

He switched to speakerphone. "What's up, Paul?"

"I thought you'd like to know that I have a line on one of the magical escapees." The hacker exhaled loudly. "He's caused considerable trouble and goes by the name Billy Crider. That's not subtle at all."

"He sounds like a good target." Daniel yawned. "More low-hanging fruit, by the sound of it."

Three quick taps sounded. "Yeah, but it's important that you get to him first. Before *they* do."

"Why?"

"He's not Oriceran or a wizard or anything but he has managed to get magic tattoos to give him power. No one quite understands how they work, only that the tats need sunlight to charge. While the Company kept him in their little hole, he was merely another human."

"I still don't understand why he's so important. I assume by 'they' you mean the rest of the Company?"

Paul sighed. "I wasn't clear, was I?"

Daniel chuckled. "Yeah, it wasn't your finest communication hour."

"Billy hasn't only caused trouble. He's traded some interesting loot."

"Interesting loot?" The agent frowned. "How interesting?"

"It has alien writing on it."

Daniel sucked in a sharp breath. "And we're sure he's a human, not an alien clone?"

Paul chuckled. "We can't be sure of anything, but he wasn't incarcerated in Level Three-E. He was with the rest of the dangerous magicals in the outer section. If he is an alien, Fortis didn't know."

"Damn. Send me all the information you have on him."

"Will do. Also, to keep you in the loop, I'm looking into Lowry and his friends, but it'll take a while."

Daniel changed lanes when an aggressive motorcyclist almost cut him off. "Fine. That's low on the priority list. If we can grab Billy, he might connect us directly to the aliens. Even if Lowry is Fortis, I doubt they know much more about aliens than we do, especially since they keep shooting first."

Paul tapped the phone three more times, a habit Daniel was now accustomed to. "I'll send the information in a minute." He ended the call.

The agent yawned once again. His eyes felt heavy and his muscles weaker than normal. He could have used a good six or seven more hours of sleep, but being bone-tired wasn't an excuse to avoid the responsibility that had shoved itself in his face.

His Company phone rang with a call from Lucy, and he once again set it to speakerphone.

"Good morning, Lucy."

"There's a detention level escapee who's come on the radar," she declared without preamble. "William 'Billy' Crider."

Daniel smirked. It wasn't like she could see him and be offended. "Oh? That's interesting. This time, can I deal with him, or does the Company have another overstaffed mission for me?"

Lucy scoffed. "No, the Company needs you to go after him."

"What's the intel?"

"He wasn't born a magical but gained abilities like damage resistance and the ability to see in the dark through magical tattoos. He's mostly used them to kill." Lucy delivered the description in a flat, almost monotone voice as if it were of no interest whatsoever.

"He sounds like a fun guy."

"If by fun you mean a violent thug who currently hurts people for no reason, then yes." She finished with a little snort of disgust.

Daniel did a quick mirror and camera check. "What does damage resistance mean?"

Lucy sighed. "Exactly as it sounds. He has magical damage resistance. They'd classify him as a level-four if he were a bounty. There are no other details."

Not such low-hanging fruit, after all.

He slowed to a stop at a red light. "Do you have information on where our not-so-friendly neighborhood thug might be?"

"Yes. The Company wants him stopped and brought back ASAP. The instructions are to tell you to handle him with the gear you already have. Based on your last report, you didn't use any of your consumables, so that shouldn't be a problem."

Daniel frowned but kept his voice casual and amused. "Oh, the Company wants him handled that quickly?"

"He's made a spectacle of himself, and it's time to end it. I'll send you the most up-to-date information available. To be clear, they want you to go after him today." Something approaching intensity seeped into Lucy's voice.

"No rest for the wicked. I'll take care of him, don't worry."

She ended the call as abruptly as always.

Daniel shook his head. As Paul had said, if Fortis had been concerned about Billy, he would have been held in Level Three-E or Hangar Twelve or whatever they wanted to call it. Even if he did have an item with an alien glyph, it might be a coincidence. Still, tasking an agent with a new mission within less than twelve hours after a previous one was unusual.

"Oh, well," he murmured. "At least this gives me a valid excuse to not be in the office today."

He turned left at the next intersection, a little disgruntled. His new CIA backup didn't provide him with regular active support, and he didn't like the idea of facing a dangerous magical with only a few hours' sleep.

Although there was one advantage to Lucy being so hands-off. It meant that he could bring in whomever he needed and the CIA would be none the wiser. He didn't need intel backup. He needed ass-kicking help he could trust, especially since he wouldn't take Billy to the CIA immediately.

The agent grinned. It was time to make a little stop at the brownstone and enlist John Rainer.

CHAPTER FIVE

Daniel pulled away from the brownstone and glanced at his companion. The man still preferred dark suits and fedoras, an outfit choice now over a hundred years out of date. Still, it worked for him, although it suggested a more dangerous copywriter vibe than a secret agent of a rogue CIA faction.

It was the hat really. Daniel rarely wore hats. Maybe that's what separated him from the older generations.

"We have about an hour before we reach his last known location in Baltimore," he explained.

John snorted. "For a guy who recently busted out of the clink, you'd think he'd keep a lower profile."

Daniel shook his head. "He got those magical tattoos when he was fifteen, killed everyone who stood in his way, then headed to Mexico a few years later. It seems he wanted to reinvent himself as a cartel enforcer. Our boy, you see, doesn't have good business sense. He merely likes to hurt people and get paid for it."

"How did he end up with some alien doodad, then?"

John patted his pocket where he'd stowed a sonic grenade, a faint look of discomfort on his face.

"He likes to trade when he needs something. Mostly, he needs crap to enable his favorite pastimes of mayhem and killing for fun. This time, at least, he confined himself mostly to gang members, which is why the local police and FBI haven't already dropped on him like a sledgehammer. We have a narrow window to grab him and figure out where he got that alien artifact."

John frowned. "I don't get it. He sounds like a basic thug to me. Back in my day, maybe being a magical thug made you special, but he's merely another ugly face now. Why did the CIA stash him in their little underground Alcatraz?"

"The CIA grabbed him when they cleaned up a few messes down south. They thought he might have good intel on Mexican magical terrorist groups, including the Red Warlocks and one particularly nasty New Veil cell down there. It turns out his intel wasn't great, but no one at the Company shed any tears over keeping a magically-enhanced killer on ice."

John snorted. "The world would probably be better off without that piece of trash."

Daniel shrugged. "Maybe, but we need him for intel, so have to take him alive. Both Paul and Lucy's background information indicates that he won't be alone. He's already managed to take over a vicious local chapter of the Hellfire Demon Disciples. He's not interested in running the gang, but they help him find easy and fun targets for murder and his other hobbies."

"Do we have to worry about bringing them in alive?"

"They have no useful intelligence. Every single one of them had to kill two people to join the gang, one man and one woman, so I won't cry if we clean Baltimore up a little in passing. That said, fewer bodies and no trail means fewer people will ask questions we don't want to answer."

John nodded. "All right. I got it. Take down the bad guys but try not to kill them if possible."

"That sounds about right. We have little information on how much punishment our guy can take. Both Paul and Lucy's information is limited to saying he's damage resistant." Daniel shook his head. "You'd think they'd want us to know more."

John shrugged. "It's not like the CIA wants to be honest about everyone in their hidden dungeon."

The lead agent nodded. "True enough, but let's be careful. We can't assume we can take him down easily."

———

A little over an hour later, Daniel chuckled as he pulled the car into an abandoned warehouse. This close to Crider's hideout, the windows along the street were heavily barred and the paint on nearby buildings was faded and peeling.

He threw his door open and stepped out. "I won't do a drone run. It'll stand out like a sore thumb in this neighborhood." He popped the trunk. "Get what you need, and I'll set up a shock fence around the car. I'd like my wheels to still be here when we get back."

The devices were highly illegal, but then again, to snatch people off America's streets and hold them in secret prisons was barely quasi-legal to begin with. The CIA had been on firmer ground when they'd grabbed Crider in Mexico.

John slipped a few more sonic grenades and magazines into the tactical vest under his jacket. "Honestly, I liked the world better when we had a few easy, big bad guys to worry about. I always thought that once we defeated the Germans and the Japanese, things would be peachy for a while. Instead, they got worse."

Daniel grinned. "Yeah, leave it to humanity to always find something nastier, and now, we have Oriceran and aliens, too."

"At least you didn't have a nuclear war while I was asleep." John shrugged.

The lead agent tossed a stun rod with a loop attached to his colleague before connecting one to his own belt. "We should expect at least a dozen gang members inside, not including the target."

The older man stepped away, and Daniel removed several black shock fence emitters and set them around the car. After he tapped a few commands into his phone, a shimmering blue field surrounded the vehicle.

Daniel tossed a few bills on the ground.

John watched in bewilderment. "What's up with the dough?"

"Shock fences aren't perfect. If you give a thief an easy win, he might take it and go away. You'd be surprised how often that works."

"Despite the fancy magic and electronic doodads, people haven't changed much, except that some have pointy ears now." The older man shook his head and adjusted his fedora. "Although it could be worse. The Nazis could be in charge."

Daniel chuckled. "Aren't you a ray of sunshine?" He nodded toward the open door of the loading bay. "Our boy's place is a few blocks away. Let's go."

The two men jogged out of the abandoned warehouse and crossed the street. A closed movie theater still had faded posters hung behind cracked glass depicting Matt Damon in a spacesuit.

"*The Martian,* huh?" the younger man muttered.

John glanced at the poster. "Is that so weird? We're hunting Martians now."

Daniel shook his head. "Nah, whoever we're after is from much farther away. I saw that movie when I was a kid; it's about an astronaut who gets stuck on Mars. It's been over twenty years since the movie came out, and even though we have portals to Oriceran, no astronauts have gone to Mars. That's a little weird."

"Elves and wizards aren't enough for you, Danny boy?"

His colleague grinned. "Call me greedy, old man. I want our space cadets on Mars, too."

They jogged into a refuse-choked alleyway. A homeless man reeking of urine slept with his head against a brick wall.

John frowned and shook his head. "You'd think that with all the abracadabra available, this kind of thing would be gone. Poor bastard."

"Maybe in another twenty years when everything's settled between Oriceran and Earth, we'll make some actual progress." Daniel shrugged. "Until then, we live with the results of human nature or even the nature of so-called intelligent beings."

They approached the end of the alley, and Daniel held his hand up in warning. John halted and felt for his pistol.

Daniel held up a chameleon ball. "According to the briefing information, it should be around this corner. We'll use this to get inside. It's a good thing we had a spare at the brownstone."

John looked at the one he'd been issued, a faint expression of distaste on his face. "I don't have a kid yet, you know."

"What does that have to do with anything?"

The older man shrugged. "I still want to have one at some point. Are you sure this thing won't zap us down there?"

Daniel chuckled. "Nope."

"Thanks for that." John snorted something close to disbelief.

"Anytime." The lead agent grinned and activated the masking device. Immediately, the light warped around him and rendered him as a hollow outline like a ghost in the alley.

The older man took a deep breath and followed suit. He hissed, dropped his ball, and winked into existence. "Sorry." He retrieved it and reactivated it cautiously.

"Try to move slowly and talk as little as possible," Daniel explained. His outline rippled with each word. "We only have a few minutes with these. It's almost impossible to remain invisible when moving fast, but we should have enough time to get inside."

The two men turned the corner under the optical

camouflage. A row of shops and stores lined the street. Several had been boarded up, but more than a few were active. People wandered casually, heading to corner groceries, laundromats, and other businesses but seemed to avoid the large bar twenty yards farther which dominated the street.

Two huge thugs with bandanas and inverted cross tattoos on their faces stood near the front with handguns tucked into the back of their pants.

"Remember, we must get inside first," Daniel whispered. "Let's find the back. Turn into that next alley."

He gritted his teeth. Time was against them, and a major firefight in the street with innocent people wasn't a risk he was willing to take. He didn't mind eliminating a few gang members, but they needed to be off the street to keep the innocent safe.

Tense seconds passed as Daniel approached the bar and turned into the narrow alley beside it. He hadn't seen anyone look their way, and a quick check behind revealed the faint distortion that defined his companion. Unlike everyone else, Daniel knew exactly what to look for.

So far, so good.

The pair headed deeper into the alley until they reached the back of the bar near a massive green dumpster. A single metal door stood in the center of a cement back porch, flanked by two windows.

"Come on. Stand near the window." Daniel moved forward and flattened himself against the wall. The air around him twitched and shimmered, and a few seconds later, he appeared. "Well, that's that," he whispered. "It takes hours to recharge."

He glanced at John, who was also now visible and simply nodded in response.

Daniel had his hand on the door when it swung open, and he jerked his hand back. It smacked against the wall on the other side. A tattooed gang member wearing a scowl stomped out, a huge black plastic bag of garbage in his arms.

"Motherfuckers," he growled. "Why don't we hire some bitch to do this shit?"

Daniel clamped his hand over the man's mouth and discharged his stun rod against his side. The gangster twitched and fell with a groan.

John grabbed the garbage bag before it hit the ground and set it aside. The CIA agent dragged the prone man away from the door and shoved him off the back porch. The stunned and drooling thug landed hard and stayed down.

Daniel flipped him over, Zip-tied him, then tied his own bandana around his mouth. They had a few minutes before he'd even twitch, but there was no reason to leave him still capable of ambushing them when he came round.

"That was close," the older man whispered.

The lead agent grinned and shrugged. He readied his stun rod and crept forward. Loud rock music and raucous voices echoed through the narrow hallway from the front. Two doors were respectively designated the bathroom and **STAFF ONLY.**

He held up three fingers with his free hand for a count-down. One dropped, then the second, and the last one snapped down as he shoved the staff door open into an empty room.

Closing it, he nodded toward the bathroom. John listened against the door for a second before he threw it open with a frown. A single urinal and an empty stall confronted them.

They continued down the hallway. Daniel slipped the stun rod back on his belt and replaced it with a sonic grenade. John mirrored him without question.

The music and voices grew louder as they approached the corner. Daniel peeked cautiously around it. The corridor continued toward the main bar, but all he could see from that angle was an empty chair.

He spun and moved to the wall on the other side before creeping forward.

"You should have seen those CIA bitches," shouted a man. "They were all crying and shit when I ripped them apart. I fucked them up like they was nothing, even more than I fucked up those losers the other day."

"I would have paid good fucking money to see that, Billy," another man responded.

Daniel suppressed a snort. For all the fury of the escape, no agency personnel were seriously hurt. That could be why IA hadn't gone nuclear on anyone they even suspected might be involved.

He reached the opening to the main floor, took several deep breaths, and readied his sonic grenade.

Billy barked out a laugh. "I would love to see some fucking CIA bitches come in here. I would fuckin' torture their asses for days and see how they like being stuck in a tiny, little—"

Daniel primed his grenade and took the corner . His eyes widened when he spotted at least two dozen gang members crowded into the bar rather than the dozen he'd expected.

Shit. Well, we're committed now.

He threw the grenade and leapt behind the wall as he drew his weapon. "They got reinforcements."

John grunted and threw his grenade a moment later. The whine of the first was immediately followed by loud groans as the pack of men succumbed, but the second didn't activate.

Bullets ripped through the wall, blasting wood, paint, and drywall over the two agents. Both ducked instinctively.

Daniel winced. "Shit. Wait. Did you forget to prime it?"

John shrugged. "Prime it? There was no pin to pull. I figured it was automatic."

"You have to slide your finger on that model and… You know what? Never mind." He yanked out another sonic grenade, primed it, and lobbed it hard against a wall, hoping for a bank shot. The moans that ensued signaled success.

The gunfire died down.

"We have to move. They won't be stunned for long." Daniel stood. "I'll run across to the other side for better vision in three…two….one." He sprinted across the open space, expecting gunshots, but all was quiet. In the main room, groaning gang members held their ears on the floor, but a shaven-headed young man stood in the center, his arms folded over his sleeveless T-shirt. Tattoos of arcane sigils blanketed his arms, along with stylized Latin calligraphy. A large Seal of Solomon tattoo covered his entire face.

"Nice look, Billy," Daniel said cheerfully.

The escapee sneered and shook his head. "Who the fuck are you?"

"I've come to take you back where you belong."

Billy snorted. "Fucking CIA. You thought that weak-ass shit would work on me?"

The agent drew his pistol and moved into the room. "It's time to go home. Or we can move you into a nice plot in the graveyard. Your choice."

The tattooed criminal cracked his knuckles and moved his head from side to side. "Fuck you. You can't hurt me, CIA. Are you coming in here with a gun? You don't know shit."

John drew his weapon. "You so sure, tattoo boy?"

Billy shook his head. A few of his men on the ground stirred. Daniel tossed another sonic grenade calmly toward them. They twitched and slumped.

The agent aimed at Billy's leg. "I don't have time for this crap."

He fired. The loud shot echoed in confined space and ripped into Billy's pants, but the bullet bounced off him and crumpled as if it'd hit thick steel. John fired a few times, but his slugs did nothing more than add semi-fashionable holes to Billy's clothing.

The thug sneered. "I said you didn't know shit."

John glanced at Daniel. "Any ideas?"

The lead agent holstered his pistol. "Stop wasting ammo." He charged the target and swung a fist.

The bastard didn't even try to dodge. Daniel's fist bounced off as pain spiked through his hand like he'd punched a brick wall. He shook it with a muttered expletive. John rushed forward and tried a few quick jabs of his own.

Billy smirked and spat on the ground. "Weak-ass pieces of shit." He reached into his boot and withdrew a long knife. "It's fun carving people up when you know they can't do shit about it."

Daniel retreated a little and scowled. "You're not invulnerable, Billy. You were rotting in that cell because someone already caught you."

"I guess they can try to catch me again after I kill both your asses." He raised the knife and stepped forward.

The agent yanked a jacket off a stunned man on the ground and swung it as Billy thrust. The jacket wrapped around the knife.

The killer grunted.

"I'll keep him busy, John," Daniel shouted. "Take him down."

The older agent yanked out his stun rod and jammed it into their adversary's side. The stun rod crackled, but the thug didn't even blink.

"Seriously?" Billy jerked the knife out of the jacket and laughed. "And here I thought I might have to worry about the CIA. You fuckers got lucky the first time you caught me."

A few men started to stir, and Daniel's heart pounded. They didn't have time to screw around. He bobbed and weaved, avoiding a few more slices and thrusts from the convict.

John circled, but the criminal remained on the offensive.

"Shooting me in the back ain't gonna work either, fucker," Billy snarled.

"That's not what I planned, pal." John took a breath and rushed forward. He clamped his hand over the man's mouth and nose and squeezed hard.

Billy's eyes widened, and he jerked the knife back to slam it into the older man's shoulder. The OSS agent hissed but maintained his hold. Daniel grabbed Billy's arm before he could stab John again.

With a quick sweep at their adversary's legs, Daniel toppled him to the ground. He dropped, pinned the thug's arm with his knee, and shoved his hand over the man's mouth.

Blood dripped from John's arm as he held Billy's body and other arm down. The thug continued to thrash in an effort to dislodge the hand blocking his breathing. The seconds ticked toward a minute, and the killer's eyes rolled back in his head.

The CIA agent released his hand, and Billy's head lolled to the side.

The OSS agent stood, wincing. "What a pansy. I can hold my breath longer than a minute."

"I'm glad to see we were on the same page. Otherwise, that could have gotten painful." Daniel released a slow breath. "Or more painful, I should say. Are you okay?"

John shrugged and grimaced, holding his shoulder. "I've had a lot worse."

Several men groaned, and their eyelids fluttered.

Daniel yanked Billy up and draped his arm over his shoulder. "Are you able to move, John?"

"Yeah. I'll slap a bandage on it in the car."

Two hours later, Daniel leaned against a brick wall in Smiling Dan's, the secret garage and equipment storage facility for the Codex team. Billy sat blindfolded and hand-cuffed to a chair with a gag in his mouth and headphones blasting white noise into his ears.

As far as the CIA was concerned, Billy had escaped.

I must be careful with reports like this. Either the Company will figure something's up, or they'll think I'm incompetent, but this is a necessary risk. We don't run across many thugs with alien artifacts.

The door opened, and Daisy stepped in, her long blonde hair swinging with each movement. Although the elf wasn't in a catsuit today, she wore tight black leather pants that looked painted on and a matching motorcycle jacket supple enough to be a second skin.

Daniel suspected magic had been involved in creating that specific look outside a comic book. He stared at her and shook his head.

She eyed him with a smirk. "What?"

"There are some very unnatural things about your clothes." He shrugged.

The elf winked. "If you can't do fun things with magic, what good is it?"

The agent chuckled as she closed the door behind her. "How is John?"

"The wound should be fine in a few days." Daisy studied their bound prisoner. "Is this the guy?"

Daniel nodded and gestured around the space. "Tim needs to think ahead more. We need something better than some unused storage room if we capture people and inter-rogate them outside the Company,"

The elf squatted beside Billy, a faint smile on her face. "Everyone's still figuring it out or making it up as they go along. But it is something to think about." She straightened and clapped her hands. Glowing sigils appeared along the top of her sleeves. "I think I have an idea how to persuade him to share the information."

"Do what you have to." Daniel shrugged.

"Oh, it's far less sinister than you think." She grinned. "Or are you into that kind of thing?"

He nodded at the prisoner. "We need the information."

Daisy rolled her eyes. "Don't be so serious. Yeah, this will hurt a little, but from everything you told me, he doesn't seem all that smart. I think we can do this another way." She stepped back and pointed to Billy. "Start your interrogation."

Daniel yanked the headphones and blindfold off. The criminal glared at him before casting a lewd gaze over Daisy's body. With a few quick movements, the CIA agent untied the gag and pulled it down.

Billy immediately spat in Daniel's face.

He wiped the spittle away with a grin. "You're the one who's tied-up, Crider. A little spit won't slow me down."

"You think you can do shit to me? Do you know how hard is to torture a person like me?" The killer grinned and licked his lips. "And you even brought me some eye candy. Oh, the things I could do to that fine piece of ass."

Daniel frowned but he resisted the urge to punch the man. He'd tried that and bullets already. Daisy rolled her eyes, clearly unimpressed, so he decided to simply follow her lead.

Let's keep this professional.

"We received word that you recently traded a small artifact, a metal card with symbols on it." Daniel used his phone to display a grainy picture taken from a drone high overhead. "All we want to know is where you sold it."

"And what? If I tell you, I walk away?" Billy snorted. "Fuck you, you piece of CIA shit. I'm gonna get out of here and bite your small dick off."

The agent shrugged. "Well, it's your choice. You can rot in a CIA black site until you die of old age or maybe, we can dump you in some crappy place where your penchant for killing will come in handy."

He slipped his phone back into his pocket and smiled. He had no intention of releasing the man. Timothy had assured him that once they'd interrogated him, Billy would be incarcerated in a secure black site, somewhere so deep even Fortis wouldn't find him.

"Fuck you. I ain't telling you shit."

Daisy sighed and stepped forward, the symbols on her arms still glowing. "You'll tell him what he wants, or I'll take the one thing from you I care about."

Billy laughed. "You gonna cut my dick off now, you Ori bitch?"

She snorted. "Why would I bother with that little stub?"

The thug's smile vanished, and he glared at her. "Watch your mouth, bitch."

Daisy shook her finger at him, her mouth curling into a disturbingly hungry grin. "You're not a true wizard or an Oriceran, Billy."

"Fuck you. I have enough magic."

"For someone with the right magic, Billy, it would be easy to disrupt the flow of power from the tattoos to your body." The elf took a step forward and leaned over the prisoner. "And then you become a sad little man who can be shot, stabbed, and killed." She pointed at Daniel. "The CIA's too afraid of magic to think of this sort of thing, but I'm an elf. We're nothing but magic."

The killer's mouth twitched, and a hint of worry appeared in his eyes. "Bullshit. You can't do that. This was special. *I'm* special. They told me that when they did this to me."

Daisy grinned and lifted her arms. The glyphs pulsed brighter, and the tattoos on Billy's arm lit up. "It's time to take all that power away, Billy. I hope you enjoy being a normal man."

Beads of sweat dotted his forehead, his breathing turned ragged, and his lip quivered. He paled.

"No, no, no," Billy pleaded. "Fuck no. Please."

Daniel watched in silence with his arms folded. Daisy's abilities were another example of why the CIA needed to get with the times and openly employ magicals. Without them, they'd quickly become irrelevant.

The elf made a few quick movements with her hand. "Ah, it's time to shred the mana cords linking the tattoos to your soul."

"All right!" Billy shouted. "I'll fucking tell you."

Daisy lowered her arms, and her glyphs faded. She smiled at Daniel and nodded to Billy.

The agent stepped forward. "Where did you sell the artifact, Crider?"

"The Dark Market." Billy shuddered. He averted his eyes to avoid Daisy. "Some elf there. I don't know his name. He was in a suit."

"Bullshit," Daniel spat. "You haven't left Earth since you escaped."

"Not the one on Oriceran, fucker." Billy chuckled, and a little color returned to his face. "There are small ones on Earth that travel to different countries. If you're in the know, they tell you where and when they'll be next."

Daniel nodded. "Okay, now we're getting somewhere. And where did you get it? The Dark Market?"

"Why the fuck would I buy it only to sell it, dipshit?" Billy snarled.

Daisy stepped forward, and he grimaced.

The prisoner sighed. "Look, I got lucky. When I broke out, I followed one of the tattooed freaks, the ones streaming from that big door farther down. I knew they were in there but never knew why or who they were. Anyway, the freak helped me escape, and I followed him for a while after that, figuring he might have something I could steal." He tried to shrug but had trouble with the motion due to his tightly bound arms. "The fucker went to some storage place. I thought he had a bunch of shit in there, maybe guns, drugs, or money. All he had was that fucking card. I knocked him around a little, thinking he was holding out, but I killed him before he said anything. At least I got the card, though."

Daniel nodded, keeping the distaste off his face. Billy was nothing but murderous scum. It was likely the alien he'd murdered was merely a victim of Fortis' overreaction.

He exhaled slowly. "We'll need the local Dark Market's next location."

The killer shook his head. "You can't go. You're normal, and they'll see that elf bitch coming from a mile away and flame her ass."

Daisy released a throaty laugh. "That would be interesting."

Daniel shrugged. "Then you have nothing to worry about, Crider. We'll be dead the minute we get near it. What do you have to lose? Except for your powers, that is."

The man's head slumped forward. "Fine, except I don't know the place." He shot a panicked look at Daisy. "But I can tell you who does."

CHAPTER SIX

A couple of days later, Daniel, Daisy, Ronni, Big Gnome, and Timothy all sat around the main table in the operations room. Madge's tiny chair was perched on top, but she had gone out to buy snacks for the group.

Daisy smiled. "We identified the location after chatting up a few of Billy's friends. It'll take place outside Trenton tomorrow."

Timothy frowned. "I'm not comfortable with you going alone."

Daniel shrugged. "The Company has nowhere to send me tomorrow. I'll say I'm meeting informants and go with her."

The older agent ran a hand over his bald head. "But you can't even see the market unless you're a magical."

"It can't be that hard. Crider's not a magical. He's merely some guy with an artifact."

Daisy shook her head. "I don't think that's true."

They looked inquiringly at her.

"I felt it when I probed his magic during the interrogation." Daisy shrugged. "I think he's a wizard who can channel his magic differently. Someone fed him a line after recognizing his potential. They probably wanted to run some experiments instead of handing him a wand and giving him proper training."

Daniel blinked. "Wait. Elves can kill a wizard's magic that easily?"

She shook her head. "No. That was totally a bluff. I merely used a little magical identification spell." She grinned and laughed. "You thought I could?"

"I'm a CIA agent, not a magical. I still have a lot to learn about magic." Daniel grunted and shrugged. "We're back to the same problem, then. The only magicals we have working for us are you, Big Gnome, and Madge. She'll probably make a lot of gnome friends at the Dark Market, but she could also very likely brag about being on a secret rogue CIA mission." He looked at Big Gnome. "I'm sorry, but I don't think I want to send you into the field."

The half-gnome shook his head. "That's fine by me. Putting my life in danger is *not* part of the Big Gnome brand, but problem-solving is."

The agent blinked as that sank home. "Huh? What are you talking about?"

Big Gnome nodded at Ronni and gave her a thumbs-up.

She smiled. "We've worked on something like this for a while because we suspected it would come up eventually. We can give you some glasses that enable you to see the market but not much more than that, and they have limited use and require extreme care. Their calibration is enormously sensitive, so you can't fight in them, for example."

Timothy rubbed his chin. "The mission isn't to take

down the market. It's to track down the source of the alien artifact. Fighting would be the last resort."

Daisy shrugged. "I'll save him if he needs help."

Daniel chuckled. "Somehow, I think I should worry more, but it sounds like we have a plan." He looked at his companions, and everyone nodded approval. "Time to visit the Dark Market."

Daniel and Daisy trekked from the dirt road toward the open field. She wore one of her standard-issue catsuits, but he had donned a black robe, complete with a wand holster.

"I look ridiculous," he muttered.

Maybe I'm closer to John's fashion preference than I realized.

The elf's blue eyes had filled with far too much excitement for Daniel's taste. "I think you look good. Most dark wizards are stereotypes. Anything else would be like a gang member in a suit."

The agent patted the wand holster and fake wand. "Maybe I should have brought a bigger wand."

She smirked. "Well, you know what they say. It's not the size of the wand that matters, it's how you use it."

"And wouldn't you like to test that out?"

Daisy licked her lips. "Be careful what you ask, Daniel. After what happened in Paris, I'm not sure if you can handle more than that."

He stared at her, and his gaze lingered on her face. Daniel was no expert on elven beauty, but the athletic blonde with her toned body checked more than a few "damn sexy" boxes by human standards. He wouldn't deny that he was attracted to her. He'd even drunkenly kissed her in Paris, although they had played it off as a joke afterward.

"You'd be surprised by what I can handle." He drew thick black glasses from a robe pocket and shook his head. "No. I'll look like an evil Harry Potter."

Daisy laughed. "Do you need a lightning scar? Of course, I wouldn't want to mess up that handsome square-jawed face of yours."

Daniel mumbled under his breath. They still had a job to do, even if a beautiful blonde elf in a catsuit flirted shamelessly with him. "I love how Ronni and Big Gnome have no fashion sense." He slipped the glasses on. "Like I was saying—woah."

She grinned. "See it now?"

A massive shimmering tent stretched a good few stories high and covered several acres from what he could see. Arcs of blue and green energy flowed across it. Double flaps in the center allowed entrance, and the wind occasionally blew them open and granted a glimpse of the people inside.

Daniel stared. "That entire thing's there, and no one but magicals can see it? What if some random elf or gnome wanders past?"

Daisy shrugged. "Who wanders for miles down a dirt road in the middle of nowhere and then heads toward an empty field?"

"Good point."

They approached the tent and Daniel shook his head. He removed the glasses and stared at the empty field before putting them back on. He rarely felt uncomfortable around magicals, but at times like this, he was reminded that sometimes, magic wasn't merely technology by another name.

How long will the CIA stick their head in the sand? There's only so much they can do with contractors.

"Let me do the talking when we get inside," Daisy whispered. "If you speak, they'll expect you to produce the entrance glyph."

Their conversations with a few other magical informants had provided the information they needed to get inside. They hoped so, anyway, but were about to find out.

Daniel nodded agreement.

They stepped through the flaps. Row after row of tables lined the massive tent. The stock ranged from the superficially mundane, such as swords, to the more exotic, including iridescent plants with fangs and twitching tendrils. Glowing orbs drifted around some tables. Elves, gnomes, dwarves, wizards, witches, and a variety of other species walked back and forth. Daniel spotted a few winged Arapaks inspecting twisted colored glass. Three rat-like Willen in silk vests gestured animatedly toward a gnome selling potions. A single dark-skinned, white-haired elf woman examined a few swords with a smile on her face.

Bright swirling clouds spun overhead. Daniel wasn't sure if they were Oricerans or some sort of decoration.

This makes the Mos Eisley Cantina look like Dullsville, USA, in comparison.

A Kilomea grunted from beyond the flap, catching Daniel's attention. The agent looked at the massive being, wondering whether they had inspired the ogres in human myths. A small wizard in a dark robe frowned beside the Kilomea, his hand already on his wand.

"Let's see it," the wizard ordered, his eyes narrowed.

Daisy lifted her hand, and a glowing, spinning glyph appeared.

Daniel's breath caught, and he carefully schooled his face into a neutral expression. He sincerely hoped to avoid a fight at the entrance to a tent filled with every manner of criminal, terrorist, and dangerous magical.

The wizard nodded. "Welcome to the Dark Market Mobile American Branch." He gestured inside. "Enjoy your stay. If you cause trouble with a vendor, we can't guarantee your safety. If you cause too much trouble, you will be banned. Or we'll simply kill you ourselves."

The agent chuckled and managed to not look as relieved as he felt. "Duly noted."

They walked about twenty feet before they spoke again. One advantage of being among so many criminals was that furtive whispers didn't seem suspicious.

"It's huge," Daniel muttered. "It could take us all day to find the vendor."

Daisy shrugged. "Do you have something better to do?"

Daniel smirked. "Better than wandering around in a giant magical tent filled with magical criminals?"

"And with me." Daisy winked.

"Fair point. Let's work our way down the rows." He shrugged and palmed his phone. "There's no harm in asking anyone if they've seen it."

The minutes turned to hours, and the CIA agent's frustration continued to build.

Daniel sucked in a deep breath and shook his head. "We've been through this entire place, and we can't find the damned thing. Maybe it's already sold. There isn't anything remotely similar here, and we can't even be certain the same vendor's present."

Daisy ran a finger over her full lips. "Maybe, but it hasn't been months since he sold it."

Two pairs of eyes watched them from a small dark tent on the corner. The table inside contained mostly pieces of metal and rock. A single green metal folding chair stood behind it. The two elves whispered to one another and pointed at Daniel.

"Huh, someone doesn't seem to like me." He nodded at the tent. "Let's go find out why."

Daisy eyed him warningly. "Don't deliberately cause trouble."

"I won't cause any trouble deliberately." The agent grinned.

His companion laughed. "Why do I have a feeling I'll have to explain to Timothy why you were turned into a toad?"

Daniel shrugged and stepped into the small tent with a wide grin. "Do you need something, gentlemen?"

The taller of the two elves sneered. "You've asked about a metal card with a strange symbol on it."

The agent nodded. "Yes. I want to buy it. That way, I'll have a matching pair."

"I don't like the look of your face, wizard." The elf narrowed his eyes.

"That's unfortunate. My mom and dad gave me this face." Daniel smiled and patted the wand holster on his right. Presumably, the elves would think he was left-handed and be surprised if he drew a hidden gun with his right. He hoped it didn't come to that, but he wouldn't die in some seedy tent.

The other elf shook his head. "Maybe we should teach you some respect, wizard."

Daisy snorted. "Human or elf, men are all the same."

The four watched one another warily, each waiting for someone to act.

The back flap of the tent opened, and an elf with slicked-back hair and wearing a dark suit stepped inside. "What the fuck is this?" he muttered. He glanced at the adversaries. "What do you got against them?"

The tall elf goon shrugged. "They've asked about that metal card the tattooed guy sold you."

The newcomer shrugged and sat in the chair behind the table. "So? What do I care? I come here to sell crap." He smiled at Daisy. "I'm Traynor. And who are you?"

"Daisy."

He laughed. "Daisy? Seriously?"

She smiled. "Do you have a problem with my name?"

"Nah, but you've gone native."

She folded her arms and gave him a thin smile. "It seems both of us have, Mr. Traynor the Suit and Hair Product Elf."

"Just saying." He waved a hand dismissively. "Sometimes, it's good to spend time with your own kind and remember what they have to offer...in a lot of different ways. Humans don't live very long, so they don't have time to develop real skills." He stared at her chest.

Daniel managed to stop himself from frowning, but it took all his willpower. It was a bad idea to piss the man in charge off when they were obviously close to a clue or even to the card itself.

He blinked in a moment of reflection.

Huh. I'm a little jealous, but we have to use whatever resource is available.

Daisy leaned forward to place one hand on the table and fluttered her eyelashes at Traynor. "I'm inclined to like men who make my day less frustrating. Your goons are right. My wizard friend and I are searching for a metal card that might have been sold here. It sounds as if you have it, or at least know where it ended up."

Traynor's gaze lingered on her a little too long before he spoke. "Yeah, I got it. Do you want it?"

Daniel nodded. "I collect them. I believe they belonged to an ancient lost Earth civilization." The lies rolled effortlessly off his tongue. Years of CIA training made it easy.

The elf man nodded. "Heritage is important, especially when you don't live that long." He leaned forward, folded his hands together, and rested his elbows on the table. "I'm not gonna bullshit you. I know if I could find a missing piece of my heritage, I'd do everything I could to get it."

"First things first." Daniel slid a hand slowly into his pocket. The two goons narrowed their eyes, but Traynor sat motionless with a grin on his face. Daniel smiled in return and withdrew his phone. "Is cryptocurrency okay, or do you prefer barter?"

Traynor snorted and smoothed his suit jacket. "I'm a modern businessman. I take Trollcoin."

The agent nodded. "Good. That's settled, then. How much do you want?"

He knew how much the elf had paid Crider for it, but he'd already shown his hand. There was no way he could expect a good price.

Traynor motioned with his hand, and a glowing yellow price appeared. "I think that's fair for my contribution to Earth's history and heritage."

Daniel maintained a cool expression even though the elf had increased the price tenfold. "That's rather exorbitant."

"This is one of those situations where you have to decide what's important to you." Traynor rested his chin in his hands, a smug look of satisfaction on his face. "Unless your little friend wants to make an arrangement. I could be convinced to cut you a discount with the right incentive."

Daisy snorted. "Please." She shook her head. "Don't think I'm impressed, Traynor. A wannabe elf prince in his tiny little tent. Come back to me in a hundred years when you've actually made something of yourself."

The taller of the elf goons glared at her and raised his arms.

His boss threw a hand up, halting the thug, and smiled the entire time. "I like you, Daisy. You're feisty, and I like feisty—a lot." He shook his head. "You're passing on a great opportunity, but so be it. I'll go ahead and knock off ten percent because I like you."

Daniel nodded. "Deal."

Nessie and Timothy would probably want to turn him

over to Fortis when they saw what he paid to recover one artifact. But at the end of the day it was merely money, and the value of the piece in their investigation and research was worth every penny.

Traynor motioned with his hand once more, and a crypto wallet address appeared.

The agent made the transfer. Thirty seconds passed before Traynor's phone beeped in his pocket.

The elf smiled. "Nice. Very nice." He burst out laughing. "You're still dumb, wizard. I don't know what you really want the card for because I don't buy your bullshit heritage story but never mind. It's not even magic. In fact, it's worthless."

Traynor snapped his fingers, and one of the goons disappeared through the rear flap. He reappeared a moment later with a small plastic tray containing a solid black metal card. Daniel's heart rate kicked up as the thug handed it over. Several alien symbols lined the top and bottom of the card.

"Don't come crying to me later," Traynor muttered, his smile fading. "All sales are final, and I don't want it back because I doubt I'll find another sucker like you. You can't do shit, either. It's not like you can call the Better Business Bureau."

Daniel forced an angry scowl on his face. "Fuck you, Traynor." He stormed out.

Daisy hurried after him.

"Next time, don't hang out with an idiot, Daisy," the elf called after them.

Once they were out of earshot, the agent dropped his

feigned angry expression and studied the card. "I guess that proves he really had no clue what this is."

Daisy shrugged. "We don't know what it is either. We merely know who made it."

He laughed. "Good point. We need to leave and get this back to the team for analysis."

CHAPTER SEVEN

The key to a good lie was to make it simple. Add too many details, and a trained CIA agent or analyst would immediately know. They could smell the lies. Daniel sat at his Company desk, working on supplemental reports regarding his confrontation with Crider.

IA hadn't summoned him again, and he'd delivered the card to the Codex team without any trouble. Thus far, he wasn't unduly concerned.

His Company phone chimed with a text from Timothy, breaking his concentration. A window popped up on his computer with the same message.

Come to my office immediately.

Daniel grimaced and stood.

Maybe IA's not done with me yet, but at least he didn't tell me to wait at my desk for them or make a run for it.

He made his way down the hall.

The door was open and his mentor sat at his desk, frowning but without his stress ball. Daniel closed the door behind him. There was no sign of Ronni's Ninja

Turtle anti-surveillance device or a silence cube. Whatever the subject for discussion, it wasn't rogue business.

The agent took a seat in front of the desk. "What did you need?"

Timothy took a deep breath and folded his hands in front of him. "There's been another Morgana sighting."

"Oh, I thought my week was too easy with only escaped magicals to worry about." Daniel sighed and shrugged. "I still don't know why she threatened me. Where was she seen this time?"

"A village on an island in the Chiloé archipelago off the coast of Chile. Forty villagers were murdered. This time, half of them had their organs harvested, and the other half were killed in a variety of...creative ways. Some look like they'd simply laid down and died in their sleep. Others were torn to pieces but without organ harvesting."

"Why?" Daniel wondered. "Why suddenly mix up her M.O?"

Timothy leaned back and studied him with a hard gaze. "You can't think of a reason? I can."

"My best guess would be that she wants to provoke someone. But who?" Daniel winced instinctively. "Are we sure it's her?"

His mentor nodded. "She left her calling card, the queen of hearts on unidentified metal." He ran a hand over his scalp in a frustrated gesture. "And I think you know what's coming next."

Daniel shook his head. "Another threat addressed to me?"

"Yes, written in a victim's blood once again. 'Daniel

Winters, where are you?'" Timothy shook his head. "She wants to provoke someone all right—you."

The agent shook his head, frowning as he considered the ramifications. "I don't get it. I've never taken on anyone called Morgana. Even if it's an alias, I've never even seen a calling card like that. I have no idea who she could be. Why the hell would she target me?"

"Your guess is as good as mine and the rest of the CIA's for that matter. Trust me. Analysts have looked deep into your background for connections, and I've seen some of their reports." Timothy shook his head. "Everyone is clueless. The only thing we know for sure is that this woman is dangerous and she's a mass murderer." His expression darkened. "We also know she's a coward and not as strong as she pretends."

Daniel chuckled with dark humor. "Why would you say that? She's killed a lot of people, Tim. That seems strong to me."

The older man turned and typed something into his keyboard. He turned the monitor to display a satellite view of a series of small islands near Chile. "She's killed in smaller towns, but nowhere near a city or anyone with decent weapons or magic. If she were confident of her power, she'd simply wander into downtown D.C. and do her thing. It means that if we can find her, we can beat her."

The younger agent snorted. "That conclusion rests on big assumptions."

Timothy shook his head. "Not assumptions. Deductions. We're the CIA. That's what we do. We gather information and deduce the truth if we can't find it directly."

Daniel sighed and scrubbed his face with his hand.

"Fine. Let's assume all we need to do is pop her with a bullet—or worst-case scenario, an anti-magic bullet." He pointed at the screen. "That doesn't solve our main problem."

A curious look settled on Timothy's face. "And what do you think that is?"

"How to find the woman? I assume we've already tried magical tracking?"

"Yes. It's brought us nothing, and we've used multiple contractors. She has a spell or an artifact that can hide her trail."

Daniel shrugged. "Have the analysts looked for a pattern in her attacks?"

"They have, but found nothing. The locations are all over the world, and there is no identifiable timing. Some intervals between the attacks are short and others long." Timothy sighed. "The truth is, we have no clue where or when she'll strike next, but some of the higher-ups have an idea how we might get her to come to us."

"Oh?"

Timothy sucked in a breath. "Like anything else in life, Daniel, it's a matter of using the right bait."

He chuckled and leaned back. "Okay, now I get it. They want to dangle me out there for Morgana?"

"Yes, but I've made it clear I won't let them order you to do this." His mentor frowned. "At the same time, I also can't think of another way to apprehend her. She'll keep killing, son."

Daniel looked down for a moment and nodded before returning his attention to Timothy. "I won't lie and say it's my all-time favorite idea, but if this woman's obsessed with me, I'm possibly the best chance we have. I'm willing to try, Tim."

The older man nodded, a satisfied look on his face. "I'll pass that up the chain. This won't happen without an actual plan, and it also won't happen anytime soon. For now, concentrate on your other work." He leaned forward meaningfully. "All of it."

Find the bad guys. Find the aliens. Find out if the aliens are the bad guys, all while avoiding another rogue CIA group. Sure, no problem. Easy-peasy.

He laughed.

Timothy blinked. "What's so funny?"

"I'm merely thinking that I'm a busy man."

Daniel rose from his desk and stretched. The meeting with Timothy had added stress to a long morning of creating fraudulent official documents. As a reward, he decided to get lunch in town rather than at the cafeteria.

He had almost reached the elevator when Troy Williams blocked his path.

The blond agent grinned. "I heard you got reamed by IA, Winters. That sounds fun, although I wouldn't know. I've never had that problem."

"If you mean I was asked a few questions and allowed to leave, then sure." Daniel shrugged. "There was a major breakout. IA needed to follow up on that. We still don't know how it happened."

Troy's face sobered, and he shook his head. "Yeah, you're right about that. We've got most of the scum, but there are still too many out there." He snorted. "And it doesn't help when you let assholes like Billy Crider get away."

Daniel narrowed his eyes. Was this another Fortis test? Timothy hadn't confirmed Troy as a member of the rogue group, but after everything the man had done, especially to Linda Hunter, Daniel would bet his shop on it.

You won't trip me up by insulting me, Troy.

"I received bad intel," he muttered. "There were twice as many gang members than I expected and I had no active support."

Troy sneered. "Weren't you a Marine? Whatever happened to adapt and overcome?"

"Bad intel kills even Marines. I'm not happy that asshole escaped any more than you are. Freaks like him on the streets put the people we're trying to protect in danger."

The other agent stared at Daniel in silence for an uncomfortably long time before some of the anger and distrust drifted away. Surprisingly, he displayed what might be concern.

Daniel said nothing. He watched in silence, waiting for his colleague to respond.

Troy shook his head. "Are you dating anyone, Winters?"

"What?"

"Are you dating anyone? I'm not asking if you're fucking, but if you're dating."

Daniel blinked. The man had caught him totally off-guard.

"Not right now," he responded cautiously. "You know how it is. We have little free time, and it's difficult to find someone you don't have to lie to." He shrugged, made wary by his companion's sudden interest in his personal life.

Troy chuckled and shook his head. "I suppose I could date some analyst or agent. Fuck, maybe even a hot contractor." He smirked. "You know, like that elf chick you run into on occasion. Dina? Darlene?"

"You mean Daisy?"

"Yeah, her. You have to admit she's got a nice body."

Daniel shook his head.

Troy laughed. "You don't think so? I know you're straight, Winters, so you can't lie and pretend indifference."

"No, Daisy's attractive." Daniel ran a hand through his hair, more than a little uncomfortable. "I...it's just— Why the hell are we even talking about it?"

Troy shrugged. "It's something I think about a lot."

"Daisy or my dating life?"

"Nope." Troy snorted. "The sacrifices we have to make. I always imagined myself as the guy with a hot wife and kids in a 'burbs house." He shrugged. "Even as an agent. Tons of agents lie to their wives and kids about what they do for a living."

Daniel nodded, happy to have moved on from his attraction to Daisy. "Then why don't you find someone?"

"Oh, I scratch an itch now and again. I'm not a goddamn monk, but what's the point of getting married? What's the point of having kids? We're always one mission away from a terrorist freak with a doomsday artifact. Before all this magic shit, at least, we only worried about stuff like nukes."

Daniel snorted. "Only nukes? How boring."

Troy frowned. "You know what I mean, asshole. The

point is, nukes leave easy trails for tech to follow. Now, all these magicals run around casting spells or making damned zombies, and that's only what we know about." He narrowed his eyes. "The world's too unstable for kids."

"The world's always been unstable. When my grandfather was a kid, global nuclear war with the Communists was the issue. A few zombies seem tame in comparison." He pointed to the other agent, then to himself. "If we do our damned jobs, the world will become more stable."

Troy nodded slowly, and a smirk crept back on his face. "Yeah, do our jobs. Like catching escaped magicals."

"Billy evading capture is a problem." Daniel pointed downward, his expression hard. "But let's face it, the real problem was the ultramax under Company headquarters—all our security eggs stashed in one basket, simply begging for a breakout."

Troy's smirk was replaced by a frown. "Yeah, Winters. You're right." He stepped past him without another word.

Daniel glanced over his shoulder as the other agent continued down the hall. He pressed the elevator call button and took a deep, calming breath.

The conversation was an important reminder. Fortis wasn't simply a group of vicious rogue agents. They were American intelligence officers doing what they thought was best to protect the country, no matter how misguided they were.

The elevator doors slid open, and Daniel stepped inside, shaking his head.

Daniel rubbed his chin as he flipped through his Dungeons and Dragons player's guide. He needed to select his character's new wizard spell for a level-up. The dungeon crawled with his D&D party and they'd netted enough scrolls for lower-level spells, but Connor had allowed him one new spell without any special justification.

He set the book down for a moment, grabbed a Ho-Ho, and took a bite. He wiped his chocolate-coated fingers hastily with a napkin and returned to perusing the guide.

Connor smiled at the group—Lorelai, Taylor, and Juan. It'd been a long time since anyone missed a session.

After a bite of yellow cake, the DM gestured at the player's character sheets. "You can't hit another dungeon tonight, but you can do town stuff while you finish leveling."

Daniel stared at the small foil-wrapped container with the remaining slice of Connor's dessert. "I think you're losing it." He pointed to the pan. "I couldn't bear to say it earlier, but now I can't help myself. Fresca cake?"

The blond dungeon master shrugged. "It has a nice citrus flavor. Besides, recent experiences have taught me to explore my world more and embrace the unexpected. You never know what mysteries or interesting things are out there." He grinned.

Subtle, Connor. Real subtle.

Daniel chuckled. The other players looked at one another and shrugged, probably blaming alcohol for the slightly odd exchange. In addition to Connor's Fresca cake, he'd drunk three Joe Blows. The CIA agent had downed a number of beers himself.

Connor, even part-time, proved to be an asset in sifting

through alien intelligence at the brownstone. Daniel wouldn't begrudge him a few humorous hints about their secret. Some secrets were painful, but this was more like a game shared by friends.

He flipped a few pages back and forth. "I'll go with *Conjure Minor Elementals*." He scribbled the spell on his worn character sheet which was due to be recopied. "Tangling with those Drow reinforced that we need more bodies to shield us sometimes. I've been too focused on a purely offensive build. Even if I can get other scrolls, my feats are too rigid."

Taylor shrugged. "You've been fine. You saved our asses tons of times in the last adventure, so it's a little late to worry about build now."

Connor whistled. "Level-eight rogue, level-seven warrior, level-eight cleric, and level-seven wizard. I sometimes forget how far this party's advanced." He laughed. "You're worried about minor build tweaks, Daniel? You guys are a machine at this point. It won't be long before each of your characters recruit a personal army. They'll need armies to stop you."

Lorelai sipped her beer. "We did grab a crapload of treasure this time. Maybe hiring a few lower-level adventurers isn't a bad idea."

Juan shook his head. "I don't want to do that. The point is our party's strength, not our management ability. What's next? We level our characters up in PowerPoint?"

Everyone laughed.

Daniel closed his player's guide and set it aside. "Before we hire a bunch of underlings, we should probably hit the adventurer's guild for our next job, but maybe that can wait until the next session."

Connor shrugged and took a bite of his final slice of Fresca cake. He chewed and swallowed before speaking. "This is a good time to ask if we want to keep these characters. It's been a good run, but I'd understand if you're ready to start a new campaign. I have some interesting ideas, but I'm fine either way."

Juan, Taylor, and Lorelai exchanged looks, but it was Daniel who asked, "Interesting ideas?"

A playful grin appeared on Connor's face. "Yeah, we tend to be so vanilla in the settings. We live in a real-life world of magic. I think we should make our role-playing a little different, more out there."

Taylor shrugged. "I'm potentially game, depending on the setting."

Lorelei scrutinized her sheet. "I can see where you're coming from."

Juan mumbled something vaguely positive as he chomped on some Doritos. His fingers were already stained orange.

Daniel chuckled, thinking about Tommy sleeping downstairs in the back room of a shop that sold magical items. Even if they weren't impressive artifacts, they still represented something most people hadn't believed were real only twenty years prior.

"What did you have in mind exactly?" he asked.

Connor's grin spread. "Spelljammer."

Of course. I should have seen that one coming.

Juan rubbed the side of his head. "Spelljammer? Isn't that the space campaign setting?"

Lorelai nodded. "Yeah. You travel in fantasy spaceships to crystal spheres containing planets and stuff. It's like Jules Verne meets Tolkien meets Jack Vance."

"D&D spells are already Vancian," Daniel pointed out. "We could take that a step further."

Taylor groaned. "I never liked Spelljammer. Combining weird alien-type science fiction stuff with fantasy is bizarre. I think aliens and elves should stay the hell apart."

Lorelai shook her head. "I think it's creative. You turn the fantasy tropes on their heads by combining them with science-fiction. It makes them both feel fresher."

Juan munched on another chip. "It's hard for me to wrap my mind around it, man."

"I don't want to do it," Taylor decided. He shook his head. "I like traditional high fantasy. The tropes have endured for decades, if not centuries in some cases because they have meaning and resonance. We don't always need new and fresh."

Daniel shrugged. "It makes me think of Clarke's Third Law: sufficiently advanced technology is indistinguishable from magic. We already live in a real-life world where technology's mixing with magic. Why not play around with it in the game, even if it's fantasy technology?" He grinned. "It's too bad aliens don't walk among all the elves and gnomes in real-life. That would be really interesting."

Connor smirked. "Yeah, it would. Aliens and elves. What a world that would be."

Taylor shrugged, apparently oblivious to the subtle jokes between Daniel and Connor. "Okay, you've convinced me to try it in the future. It does sound kind of interesting, but that doesn't mean I'm ready to give up on this character."

Juan nodded his agreement, and Lorelai shrugged.

Connor lifted his fourth Joe Blow and gulped down the rest of the Fresca-enhanced alcoholic drink. "Duly noted. I'm more than happy to keep the current campaign for another year." He exhaled and set his drink down. "Though I don't think I can DM anything else tonight."

Daniel smiled. "I think we focus on buying equipment and finish leveling up."

Juan cleared his throat. "If we're wrapping the game up, I think a little For Want of a Dollar is in order."

They looked eagerly at him.

He smiled and tapped his forehead. "Have any of you heard of Project Starlight? Back in the day, the government types tracked magicals in the entertainment industry." Juan rolled his bag of chips closed. "A big part of that was Project Starlight. They were worried about things like Light Elf singers using songs to control people and that kind of thing so kept track of famous people, entertainers, and socialites."

Daniel chuckled. He knew about multiple secret government projects involving aliens, but somehow, he'd never heard about Project Starlight. Judging by the looks on the others' faces, they hadn't either. They confirmed it with a shake of their heads.

Juan rubbed his hands together. "Then let's do our first challenge. One family had considerable fame in the early 2000s for show-business stuff. But they had other famous members before and after that, and still do even today, despite all the Oriceran stuff that makes it harder to achieve. Recently declassified PDA documents about Project Starlight indicate that several of the women in the family are witches, and they've used magic to help their careers. I'll bet one dollar against each of you that you can't guess who they are. I'll list four names, and you can choose one."

Lorelai groaned.

"Hey, next bet, you decide the subject." Juan shrugged.

She rolled her eyes. "Fine. Bring it on."

Daniel, Connor, and Taylor all nodded and leaned forward expectantly.

Juan spread his arms like a prophet about to deliver divine wisdom. "The Singhs, the Lees, the Hiltons, and the Kardashians. Write down who you think it is and pass it to me. That way, we don't have any bias."

Daniel ripped paper from his scratch pad and scribbled his answer: the Singhs. He wasn't an expert on non-spec fic pop culture, but even he'd seen a few of the recent movies starring a Singh sister or two. He wasn't sure if their worldwide fame dated back to the early 2000s but recalled reading that the family had been in acting for four generations, although they didn't do Hollywood films until recently.

Everyone folded their papers and slid them forward. Juan made a show of opening each and nodded sagely.

He cleared his throat. "We have one correct answer." He raised his finger slowly to point at Connor.

Daniel groaned, Taylor scowled, and Lorelai chuckled.

"Care to share with the class, man?" Juan asked.

"The Kardashians," Connor explained.

Juan nodded. "Yep. From what I saw in the Project Starlight files, they specialize in life magic."

"That's how I knew." Connor stood with a triumphant smile. "All the younger ones have shows, maybe a half-dozen of them on the net. The matriarch, Kris, is in her eighties now but doesn't look a day older than sixty. She says it's good plastic surgery."

Daniel eyed Connor expectantly. "So she used life magic to look younger but she didn't stop the aging originally?"

"She already looked way younger in her sixties." Connor shrugged. "I think she's used it for a while."

The CIA agent shook his head. "Maybe the people who should really worry about magic are plastic surgeons."

CHAPTER EIGHT

J ake sighed and walked with deliberate slowness. His cloaking field would render him completely invisible unlike the primitive version the humans used, but with fast movement, the secondary effects around him could be noticed. He'd already kicked a rock into a man's leg by accident.

He looked at the upstairs apartment, then at the sign in front. Rooney's Antiquities and Oddities. The day before, his tracker had followed residual energy patterns to the shop, which meant there was almost certainly technology made by his people inside. This was consistent with what he'd found in searches at the brownstone and with other data his superiors had sent him.

Daniel's movements had correlated with the discharge of a transformation gun, but neither location contained the weapon. The guns weren't at the brownstone, which left a few other places to check.

It was proving difficult to recover the missing weapons. His people's operatives had limited freedom of movement.

The CIA agent might have more advanced technology inside, so it was necessary to check. No human should have something so powerful.

The real problem was to find a time when there wasn't at least one person in the building. His disguise as a human child effectively deflected suspicion, and he could disable the cameras easily enough, but if he were seen and described, the CIA agent would immediately deduce that Jake wasn't the amnesiac human child he appeared to be. As it was, he took a huge risk using the tactile holoprojector decoy of him asleep at the brownstone during his jaunts outside.

Jake wandered to a patch of shade beneath a tree and knelt near the massive trunk. He confirmed no one else was near with a quick glance and activated his communicator. It would disrupt the cloaking field, but he needed orders. His actions could have major consequences.

Rather than risk being overheard, he glided his finger over the device and the haptic input sent off his written message quickly in his native language.

At Winters' home and shop. Technology signatures inside, but one elderly human present. Attempted entry this morning, but the human grandfather and an adolescent half-elf were present. A strong possibility remains that the transformation guns are inside. Request orders concerning immediate afternoon infiltration.

He waited and considered the options. If Daniel withheld knowledge of the guns from his friends, it could mean he planned to use them and that he wasn't the friendly hero he played at the rogue headquarters.

It didn't matter. The humans couldn't be trusted and were vicious and violent. Both the CIA and foreign agencies had proven that repeatedly. Just because Daniel opposed Fortis didn't mean he was good. He claimed to want to prevent war but hoarded weapons in preparation for one.

Jake snorted. No. He wouldn't let a friendly face fool him.

His communicator activated and the response streamed across the holographic display.

Report acknowledged. Hold position. Wait for night entry. Do not attempt night entry if Daniel Winters is present, but we consider the grandfather and adolescent acceptable infiltration risks. Remember your orders. Recover the transformation guns but do not harm any non-hostile civilians.

Jake snorted. Non-hostile civilians? Was there such a thing on Earth?

He responded quickly.

Orders received. Falling back.

The alien deactivated the communicator and reactivated his cloaking field. He now merely needed to wait.

Peter yawned and stretched as he sat up in bed. He rubbed his eyes and looked at the clock on his nightstand. 1:32 A.M.

He should have gone back to sleep but stood instead, grabbed a robe from his doorknob, and slipped it on. His throat and lips were parched, and he could use the kind of relief that only a certain grapefruit-flavored beverage could provide.

It was late-night Fresca time.

The old man tied his robe and opened his door. He crept down the short hallway toward the living room and kitchen. Daniel's door was still open, and the bedroom was empty. His grandson had mentioned having to stay late at the Company to catch up on some reports.

Peter stopped and furrowed his brow as he heard a faint buzzing noise from downstairs. It paused and sounded again, then stopped. He'd lived in the apartment and run the shop for decades so knew every floorboard's squeak and the hum of the vents. Whatever that noise was, it came from inside the building downstairs, but he had no idea of the source.

He sighed and shook his head. It could be Tommy, but the boy didn't usually get up in the middle of the night. When he did, his footsteps and the creak of the back room door were distinctive enough for the older man to recognize.

Daniel said the Company broke in before. Are they here again?

Peter stood motionless for a few seconds before he hurried back into his bedroom and yanked open a dresser drawer. He retrieved a stun rod from beneath his underwear.

He might not be as strong and flexible as he once was, but he could still defend his property and the boy. He also had a gun in the closet but didn't like the idea of firing bullets around in the dark.

Abandoning stealth, he threw the apartment door open

and tromped down the stairs. His heart thumped a little harder than a tired old man's should.

He heard the buzz again. This time, it was louder and sounded like it came from the basement.

Peter hurried down the steps, and his stomach knotted. He rushed toward the back room, threw the door open, and raised the stun rod. The darkness hid the shelves, tables, and Tommy's cot.

After a deep breath, the old man flipped the lights on and prepared to charge whatever bastard had broken in. No intruder materialized, not even a dumb teen criminal looking for an easy score. The unconscious half-elf groaned and rolled to his side in a sleeping bag.

Peter chuckled. "Nothing wakes up you up, huh, kid?" He knelt beside the cot with a groan and shook the boy gently with his free hand. "My knees are too old for this."

Fifteen seconds passed before Tommy's eyes—one gray and one light blue—flickered open.

He blinked, and his eyes widened. "Woah." His gaze cut to the stun rod. "You said I could have that Fresca even though you only had three left, dude."

Peter grunted and stood, brandishing the stun rod. "This isn't for you, Tommy."

The boy rubbed his eyes. "What's going on?"

"I heard a weird noise." The old man nodded toward the door to the main shop. "Time to get up. I need you where I can see you, so I know you're safe."

Tommy unzipped the sleeping bag and swallowed. "Maybe we should call the cops?"

"It might not be anything. I don't want to waste their time."

He also didn't want to risk ruthless Fortis agents murdering some innocent cop who stopped by in response. If necessary, Peter could slow any intruders down long enough for Tommy to escape.

The elf scrambled out of the bag, his Spider-Man pajama bottoms hanging low. "Do I get a cool weapon, too?"

"When you're older, sure." Peter nodded toward the basement door. "Open that. I'll go down first."

The teen hurried to it and took a deep breath. His hand hovered over the handle like Indiana Jones ready to swap out an idol. He shoved the door open and raised his fists. "Bring it, bitches."

"Don't talk like that, boy." Peter chuckled and shook his head.

No CIA agent or thugs rushed up the stairs.

He turned the basement lights on and jogged down. A few tools sat on his workbench, along with the 3D printer in the corner, but there was no sign of an intruder. Nothing suggested that anyone else had been there since his last visit. The vault remained concealed behind the wall. He reminded himself not to check with Tommy there.

He looked slowly around the room, and his gaze paused at the corner.

"What is it?" Tommy asked quietly from behind him.

Peter leaned forward. Something about the shadows unsettled him, but he shrugged it off. His old eyes had failed him more than once. "I'm seeing things, I guess. Let's check upstairs."

Ten minutes of searching revealed nothing in the rest of the shop. As far as either of them could tell, no one was inside and no one had broken in. Everything was where it should be, and the alarm systems and cameras all functioned normally.

Tommy leaned against the counter and yawned. "Looks like we're not gonna get stabbed in our sleep, dude."

Peter frowned. "I could have sworn I heard something."

"You probably heard a cat outside, or maybe it was a dream. Should we tell Daniel?"

The old man shook his head. "He has enough on his plate and doesn't need to worry about my old ears playing tricks on me." He sighed and set the stun rod on top of the counter. "Half the time, I'm hard of hearing, but suddenly, I hear too much." He ran a hand through his thick silver hair. "Don't get old. The experience and wisdom are nice, but the hearing and knees are a killer."

"I'm a half-elf. It's gonna take me longer."

Peter grinned. "Well, we're both up, and I figure it'll take us a while to get asleep.

Tommy looked confused. "Yeah?

"I have two Fresca left, and you have two cinnamon Pop-Tarts. It sounds like a good snack to me."

Tommy grinned. "Great minds think alike, Mr. Rooney."

———

Jake flattened his back against the wall in a nearby alleyway, and his heart raced at the thought of his narrow escape. The old man had looked directly at him as if he could see through the cloaking field. For all Jake knew, the half-elf had magic that could see through it although he hadn't appeared to notice him.

He transmitted a new message.

Transformation guns verified via scan to be inside the building. They're stored in a subterranean vault. I received a system ping from one of them but not the other so perhaps they disabled it somehow. I'm unsure how to get into the vault undetected, since security is much tighter than anticipated.

Jake waited in the darkness. He lacked the equipment to break into the vault and would need considerable time to circumvent the defenses, but he would follow orders. Perhaps Winters had some explosives hidden in the building.

His communicator lit up with a response.

Report acknowledged. Withdraw for now. Wait until suspicion has died down. Winters isn't the only threat. Fortis might be watching his shop as well.

Jake released a breath he hadn't realized he was holding and replied.

Orders received. Withdrawing for now.

CHAPTER NINE

Daniel gulped the warm brew that Tommy brought for him in his Green Lantern mug. Without caffeine, he'd be little more than a log-shaped human for the day. He'd stayed up until 3:30 working on more Crider-related reports, which seemed a worse punishment than having assassins come after him. He half-wondered if Fortis tried to wear him down through bureaucratic warfare—a truly diabolical plan.

He slammed the mug down and scowled at the masked Kyle Rayner on the side. "I need a ring to help with my reports. I wonder how much paperwork a Green Lantern has. I bet Hal Jordan enjoyed doing it when he was a Green Lantern."

Tommy laughed. "Is that what you were doing the other night? Mr. Rooney said you weren't out of town."

Daniel shrugged. "Yeah, I had some paperwork to finish for new items I'll ship here soon. Customs is a bitch when you deal with magical items."

He hated lying to the boy, but the last thing Tommy

needed was to be swept into the world of the CIA or aliens and rogue factions. If Daniel did his job properly, people like Tommy would never even know of the threats.

The teen opened his mouth like he wanted to say something but shut it and smiled. It felt forced to Daniel.

"What's wrong?" he asked. He finished his coffee, and a little of the heaviness lifted from his eyes. Who needed magic when you had caffeine?

"Nothing's wrong." Tommy shrugged. "Why would you think that?"

Daniel leaned forward and locked eyes with the boy. "You seem like you have something to say, for one thing, but also because you basically live here now. I've thought about that for a while."

Tommy blinked. "T-that's what you're worried about? You want me gone?"

"No. You've missed the point. I'm not worried… Actually, yeah. I am, but not because I want you to leave. There's a reason why you're living here, and it isn't so you can read rare comics before you go to bed. I need you to be honest with me, Tommy. Does your father hit you?"

Daniel stared at him, watching his face and body for tells.

The young man scoffed. "Nah. He doesn't hit me or scream at me or whatever else you think. He's not like that. He's okay."

The CIA agent shook his head. "Then why do you stay here so much? I don't mind, and we have the room, but a boy should be with his parents or one of them at least."

"He's not a bad guy or anything. Seriously, dude. He's

just a…musician." Tommy sighed and slumped against the counter.

"A musician?" Daniel folded his arms. "And what does that mean exactly? What does his job have to do with it?"

"He's got a job with responsibilities. You don't want him to be a bum, right? A man who can't provide for his family is no man at all."

Daniel frowned. "The first responsibility a father has is to his son. I still don't follow, though. What do you mean by responsibilities? And why would that make you stay here?"

Tommy straightened with something approaching pride on his face. "You ever heard of Trevilsom?"

"Yeah. It's a prison. The Oriceran version of an ultramax—the ultimate prison." He groaned. "Please tell me your father didn't serve time there."

They didn't throw minor tax cheats in Trevilsom. It was the kind of place where they incarcerated felons like the dangerous Atlantean war leader Rhazdon. If the half-elf's father was a former inmate, he very likely shouldn't even be on Earth, let alone raising a teenage boy in Alexandria.

The teen's eyes widened, and he laughed. "What? My dad serving time? No. He wouldn't last five minutes. I don't mean the prison. I mean the death metal band."

Daniel blinked. "Death metal band?"

I'm now so lost in this conversation, I need GPS to get me back on track.

"Yeah." Tommy bobbed his head. "My dad is their new drummer." He lifted his hands, made horns with his fingers, and whipped his long hair back and forth.

"Never heard of them. I'm more of a rock guy than a metal guy."

"They are a semi-big deal because they've got both humans and elves," Tommy explained. "They aren't the first mixed-species band, but there aren't many Light Elves in metal. They do mostly pop and classical, plus that country chick."

Daniel rubbed the back of his neck, utterly baffled. "Okay, so your dad is in a metal band, and what? He practices so loudly you have to sleep here?"

Tommy shook his head. "He's tried to make it big for as long as I can remember, and he finally has. Now, he's on the road with Trevilsom, touring with Black Sabbath Reborn and the Sons of Gwar."

"Black Sabbath Reborn? I have heard of them. They have that necromancer who claims he's Ozzy Osbourne in a new body."

The youngster nodded with a grin.

The agent frowned, processing everything as the pieces fell into place. "He's on tour with these big deal bands but left you at home. Your mom's long gone, so you're…sitting home alone." He sucked in a breath. "Damn it."

Tommy waved dismissively. "Yeah. I'm not a baby or anything, dude, but it's weird being there alone all the time. I prefer to sleep where there are other people." He looked down and scraped the bottom of his shoe against the linoleum. "So, I stay here."

Daniel ran his hands through his hair and pushed back the irritation. "So, what? When you're not here, you don't eat?"

"No, no, no. My dad's not like that. He bought a crap-ton of Ramen cups before he left. Yeah, I get tired of eating the stupid stuff all the time, but that's another reason I come over here—especially since Mr. Rooney buys me snacks like Pop Tarts." He lifted a shoulder in an expressive shrug. "It's not a big deal. The tour will finish soon, and he'll be back."

The agent forced a smile, even though his pulse thundered in his ears. Tommy needed his father more than ever because his mother had abandoned them. A teen shouldn't have to rely on other people to make sure he did what he had to for his future, like going to school or eating a damned non-ramen breakfast.

"You should head to school, Tommy. I don't want you to be late, and I know I slept in." He nodded toward the door. "But I feel better now that I understand the situation," he lied.

"Thanks, I didn't mean for it to be a big mystery." Tommy saluted mockingly and hurried out the door.

He watched the boy until he disappeared around the corner of a building.

I need to have a conversation with a certain drummer the second he gets back.

Daniel pushed into Nessie's office with a frown on his face. As much as he'd tried to push his anger at Tommy's father aside, it festered on his way to work. Even his superior's text instructing him to come to her office for a mission briefing when he arrived didn't quell his frustration.

Is this my resentment toward my parents for disappearing

because of work? I don't know, but they didn't choose to disappear, unlike Tommy's dad.

Nessie looked up from her computer and nodded. "This should be a straightforward mission. I'm sure that'll be a welcome change of pace."

Daniel dropped into a chair, still frowning. "Straightforward?"

She nodded, withdrew a briefcase from beneath the desk, and set it on top. "Yes. So much so that your loadout will be minimal. Chameleon ball, directional EMP, multiple stun pins, electronic and physical lockpicks, sonic grenades, and AR glasses. Standard ordnance. One drone. We don't anticipate significant magical resistance despite the overall danger." She pushed the briefcase toward him.

"Will the charming Lucy provide any active backup or merely bust my balls afterward?"

Nessie arched an eyebrow and pursed her lips. "Active backup has been authorized in this case. Not only that, the Company's concerned about the relative danger, so you also have direct backup. They don't feel a contractor is trustworthy for this particular mission."

Daniel frowned. "It's so straightforward that I have active backup and another field agent to assist?"

"That's an accurate summary, yes." Something approaching irritation flashed in her eyes. She cleared her throat. "Let's discuss the details, and you'll understand their concerns."

"Okay, what or who am I going after?"

Nessie turned her screen to face him, revealing a picture of an elaborate, bejeweled, multi-tiered golden crown. "This artifact is the Crown of Poseidon. We do know it was originally Minoan, but details of its provenance aren't verified."

Daniel nodded. "So it's not merely a pretty hat?"

"If only." The director pressed a key, and the screen image changed to several collapsed and damaged buildings in the middle of a desert. "The crown can cause earthquakes even where there are no fault lines. This is a nightmare scenario, Daniel. It's a magical weapon of mass destruction, and you don't even have to be a magical to use it."

The agent narrowed his eyes to focus on the rubble, debris, and bodies. "And where is it now?"

"In a dacha outside Moscow owned by one Viktor Mikhailov." She tapped a key, and a picture of a balding, middle-aged man in an ill-fitting gray suit filled the screen.

He gestured toward it. "He's not simply a man who collects ancient artifacts for museums, I assume."

Nessie shrugged. "He might be a collector, but he also happens to be a high-level member of the Russian Mafia. For the last few years, he mostly ran their operations in Hungary, but he's recently relocated to Russia. Our information suggests his acquisition of the crown played a role in his decision to return to his homeland."

"If he's so bad, why don't the Russians move against him? I can't imagine they'd trust a random mobster with an earthquake artifact."

She sighed. "Those who would care don't know he has it. In addition, he's tied to certain dangerous factions within the government who might be deliberately withholding the information from the others. If those factions are involved, it complicates matters for us."

"Meaning?"

"You need to minimize casualties unless absolutely necessary, or we risk a major international incident. As it is, we're sending CIA agents to steal…that is, *recover* an artifact on Russian soil rather than partnering with the locals." Nessie turned her screen once more. "You can imagine how they'll react if they figure out who's responsible, even without a trail of bodies."

"Has anyone thought to spill the beans to those Russians with a less vested interest in a mobster with a WMD and let them do the raid?" Daniel shrugged.

Nessie pursed her lips. "That presents other difficulties. It's important that Mikhailov not have the object, but it's almost as important that the Russian government not get it either."

Daniel smirked. "You're talking peace through superior artifact power."

"Yes." She nodded emphatically. "We can't allow an artifact gap with any nation or kingdom on Earth. It'll take time to match Oriceran countries, but we have to start somewhere."

"So, go in, grab the crown, and don't kill anyone if possible, but I'll have Lucy and a partner." Daniel looked to the side for a moment. "And who will I work with?"

Nessie took a deep breath. "Troy Williams."

Daniel chuckled. He stood and closed the door before activating his silence cube. He didn't have the time or patience for games. "Are we sure this isn't a Fortis trap?"

"No, we're not." Nessie shrugged. "Tim's looked into it, and he doesn't believe it is, but he also admitted that he can't be sure. There's some minor operational concern higher up due to your *failure* to bring in Crider, but we cannot pull Williams off this case without raising considerable suspicion. If it means anything, I also doubt it's a trap."

"And why is that?"

"Because if that's the case, it makes no sense to have an active backup. There's no indication Lucy works for Fortis, and even if she did, there are too many data streams. They make it difficult to cover up malfeasance and would leave a big trail leading right to Williams and them. They can try and kill you anytime they want over here." She shrugged.

"Comforting."

"The truth rarely is."

Daniel scratched his eyebrow, deep in thought. "Okay, so hit the dacha, steal the crown, don't kill anyone, and make sure Troy doesn't shoot me in the back while I'm at it."

Nessie gave him a curt nod. "An excellent summary."

He snorted. "Company business trips are always fun."

Troy grinned as the two CIA agents made their way through a dense line of pine and spruce that formed a natural barrier behind the dacha. The trees stood close enough to deny easy access to most large vehicles and blocked most of the starlight from above.

"What's so funny?" Daniel asked, peering at the other man. The AR glasses' night-vision mode allowed him to see Troy easily enough. The green tint and eerie reflection in the man's eyes gave him a sinister cast. The ski mask and dark fatigues made them look like terrorists.

Troy shrugged. "We could have had to do this shit in the middle of the winter." He smirked. "Then it'd be Winters in winter."

Daniel chuckled. "I suppose it would. How are we doing, Lucy?"

"No unusual activity on thermal," she reported, her voice flat and almost monotone through their earpieces. "As far as I can tell, there are eight men in the building, but only two are moving. I can't get the drone any closer. Our intel suggests a five-hundred-foot anti-drone kill zone. If I try to disable that system, I risk tripping the alarms. It's touchy and borderline as is."

Daniel ducked under a low-hanging branch. "And the timing on the motion sensors?"

The woman scoffed. "The system won't reset for an hour. You should have plenty of time."

She might not be friendly, but she can do the job. I'll give her that.

Troy tromped forward, setting a quick pace. "Don't worry." He glanced over his shoulder at Daniel. "This will be over well before then."

Is that a threat, Williams? I'll die someday, but it won't be outside a rich mobster asshole's summer home.

After a few more minutes, the outline of the dacha appeared in the distance, a vast, elaborately gabled, two-story structure. Their intelligence indicated that the crown was most likely kept in the basement.

"No external guards spotted," Lucy reported. "There are still two roving guards, one on each floor. Motion sensors are still down. I'll initiate camera spoofing once you're ready."

Daniel examined the ground between the tree line and the building. "We have a lot of open ground to cover. The chameleon balls would work, but if we're running, they might see a distortion, even in the dark."

Troy snorted. "Don't be such a pussy, Winters."

Lucy cleared her throat. "I'll let you know when the guards are on the opposite side. That should reduce the risk."

"Thanks, Lucy," Daniel replied. "That's a little bit more actionable than 'don't be a pussy.'" He drew his chameleon ball from a vest pouch.

Only the occasional rustle of wind or hoot of an owl broke the quiet as they waited. It would have been a serene experience if they didn't have to infiltrate a guarded building to steal a WMD artifact from a mobster.

Lucy cleared her throat. "Both guards are now on the opposite side but hurry. I noticed movement from a couple of the others. It could be a shift change, but there will be four active guards soon either way."

"Fucking wonderful," Troy grunted.

Daniel activated his chameleon ball and disappeared into the darkness. "Remember, we have to keep this non-lethal."

"If possible," Troy replied, activating his.

Both agents raced forward, their outlines shimmering in and out of focus in the dark of the rural Russian field. They closed on the house and stopped at a side door. No alarms or yelling men greeted them, a good start.

"Based on your current location," Lucy advised, "when you enter, turn right and locate the stairs to the basement."

Daniel deactivated the chameleon ball to save the

charge in case he needed it later. Troy reappeared behind him.

A keypad lock secured the door. Daniel waved his electronic lockpick over the mechanism. After a few seconds, it released with a click. He nodded to his partner, who readied a stun pin.

Daniel pulled the door open slowly and crept inside, wincing in the bright light. He tapped the side of his glasses to revert to normal vision

"They obviously have only the bedrooms dark at night." He pulled a sonic grenade from his tactical vest. "Let's do this."

The wood creaked beneath his heavy boots as he moved inside with Troy right behind him.

This would be a good time to shoot me in the back.

Lucy hissed. "Something's wrong."

"Wrong?" Daniel's whispered urgently. "That's not what I want to hear as I enter a guarded dacha."

"I've lost the drone. The feed went dead. An EMP I think, and they know something's wrong as they've rebooted the system. You have about five minutes at the most."

Troy grunted. "Fucking great. Let's grab it and go."

Daniel raced down the hall, no longer concerned about noise. He spotted the stairs with relief. At least something was going right. He picked up the pace and paused before descending.

Troy charged toward him, an angry look on his face and the stun pin in his fingers.

What the fuck? Was he waiting for this?

Before Daniel could grab his gun, the other agent jerked

his arm and threw the device. Daniel gritted his teeth, but the pin continued past him. A buzz sounded, followed by a groan and a thud.

He spun, saw one of the suited guards twitching on the ground, and looked over his shoulder. "Thanks, Williams"

"You owe me, Winters," Troy smirked.

"I'll buy you a beer at Lucky's." Daniel Zip-tied the guard quickly.

A shrill alarm shrieked through the dacha.

"So much for five minutes." He grimaced. "And so much for stealth. Keep watch out here. I'll grab the crown." He charged down the stairs.

Troy yanked out a sonic grenade and another stun pin. "Hurry your ass and make sure it doesn't get away like Crider did."

Daniel laughed as he reached the bottom and looked around the furnished basement for a hidden safe—maybe behind one of the book or trophy cases, he decided.

Arrogance could be annoying, but tonight, it saved the CIA agents the effort of a real search.

Viktor had placed the artifact on a fancy silk pillow on top of a podium rather than behind a DNA-locked vault or bulletproof glass. A little plaque beside it even explained that it was the Crown of Poseidon in both English and Russian.

"You arrogant son of a bitch," the agent muttered.

"Fuck you, Winters," Troy growled over the comms, though it was almost drowned out by the loud alarm. "I saved your ass."

"I meant Viktor."

"Sure you did."

Lucy sighed. "Everyone's converging on your location."

Several gunshots rang out.

"Hurry your ass up, Winters," Troy barked. "It'll be your damned fault if I have to go lethal on them."

Daniel shook out a mylar bag, shoved the crown in without ceremony, and tied it to his belt.

At least they didn't have to shoot their way out at ground level. A single door led out of the basement.

"There's a way out down here."

Troy threw a sonic grenade. Several men yelled in Russian, and their voices echoed into the basement. The agent sprinted down the stairs and paused briefly to throw another grenade.

Daniel ripped the basement door open and ran into the next room. Motion-sensitive lights clicked on. Motorcycles, electric four-wheelers, and a solar dune buggy were parked inside the garage which had an angled concrete ramp to the surface.

"I found our way out," he yelled.

Troy rushed in and slammed the door closed. Bullets tore through the wood.

He ducked and sprinted to a four-wheeler. "Let's get the hell out of here. Thank you, Viktor, for push-button ignition." He ground the starter button down, and a light beep signaled the electric engine powering up.

Daniel mounted his own vehicle. "The garage door has an electronic lock. Can you get it open, Lucy?"

She heaved an annoyed sigh. "Give me a minute."

"We don't exactly have a lot of time," he replied, his tone curt.

More bullets blasted through the door and the wall

followed by the sound of heavy footsteps in the other room. Troy had stunned a fair number of guards but clearly not enough.

Daniel drew his gun as the door to the basement burst open. A man with a rifle shouted in Russian and aimed at Troy. Daniel fired two quick rounds into his leg. The Russian man screamed and fell, and his rifle clattered to the concrete floor.

"Got it," Lucy exclaimed.

The garage door rose. Daniel continued laying down cover fire. The Russians tried to return fire through the wall without daring to peek around the corner and managed only to destroy their employer's vehicles. The wounded guard crawled around the corner, moaning.

I hope I didn't just cause an international incident.

Troy's four-wheeler zoomed forward. He ducked, and avoided a scalping by mere inches. Daniel gunned the throttle to follow him. He rode the brakes and spun the vehicle to the side a few seconds later.

"What the hell are you doing?" Troy barked ahead of him.

"Covering our asses." Daniel yanked out a directional EMP, aimed the long black tube at the garage, and activated it. The device buzzed and hissed. "That should hold them for now. Let's go."

Troy grinned. "Good thinking."

The CIA agents roared away as several guards rushed from the garage and opened fire. The bright muzzle flashes lit up the night and loud reports shattered the serenity of the wilderness outside.

"You still got the crown?" Troy asked. "Because otherwise, that was a big waste of time."

"Yes. Safe and secure." Daniel patted the bag bouncing on his thigh.

"You're not so bad, Winters, even if you did let Crider get away. At least when it comes to artifacts, you know what you're doing."

Daniel chuckled. "Same to you."

His smile faded, and he was glad Troy was focused on driving and missed his partner's sudden frown.

Everything he'd said to Troy was true, but he couldn't ignore the fact that this same man had participated in the brutal torture of Linda Hunter. Just because a Fortis agent was good at his day job didn't make him a good man.

Of course, he probably thinks the same thing about me.

The gunfire died down. For that night, the two men were on the same side, and that would have to be enough.

CHAPTER TEN

The mission had gone well, although Daniel still struggled with jetlag. He stepped off the elevator and into the operations room at the brownstone. Despite him wounding a man, the Russians hadn't complained or even mentioned the raid. From what Timothy told him, the government was relieved that the crown was no longer in the country.

Jake sat drawing at the main table, this time with colored pencils. Madge relaxed in a pixie-sized chair on the table with her legs crossed and a tiny magazine in her hands. Her wings twitched as she turned the page.

Daniel looked at the page. Presumably, the subject was Madge although it resembled a potato with wings. Then again, that was a fairly accurate rendering of the pixie.

The boy smiled at Daniel. "Hello."

Madge waved but didn't look up from her magazine.

Daniel pointed to Jake's art. "That's a nice picture. Much better than I could do at your age."

The pixie nodded quickly. "It captures my essence," she explained, her voice as deep as ever.

Jake gathered his pencils. "Thank you." He yawned. "But I'm gonna go take a nap now." He waved and walked toward the elevator and Daniel frowned as he watched him leave.

Madge looked over the edge of her magazine. "I wonder if the aliens messed with him somehow."

"They did kidnap him. That's messing with him."

"I mean more than that, hon. Changed him or something."

Daniel frowned. He didn't respond immediately but waited for the elevator doors to close. "What do you mean?"

The overweight pixie shrugged. She closed her magazine, fluttered into the air, and placed it on her chair. "He's tired all the time, and he sleeps all the time. The other rescued humans weren't like that."

Daniel stared at the elevator, his thoughts churning. "It's probably a symptom of depression. It'd be hard for anyone to adjust to what happened, let alone a child. They've run tests, though. He seems healthy, and there's no genetic damage."

Madge pushed her cat's eyes glasses up her nose. "I don't know what to tell you, hon, except what I've seen. He still sleeps away almost half the day."

"Well, maybe I'll talk to him later." Daniel frowned. Something pricked at the back of his mind. His instincts told him there might be more to worry about than depression.

Maybe he needs more time to adjust. I hope that's it. What else could it be?

He turned toward Madge. "Wait. 'Weren't?'"

The pixie arched an eyebrow and folded her arms as she bobbed in the air. "Huh? Don't blurt out random stuff, Daniel."

"No. It's what you said. You said the other humans *weren't* like that, not aren't. Did something happen to them?"

She shook her head. "No. Yes. Yes and no."

Daniel stared at her. "Are you drunk?"

Could pixies even get drunk?

Madge smirked. "You couldn't handle me if I were. What I mean is that Tim got rid of them." She waved airily. "No, that's too harsh. Resettled? They all agreed to keep their mouths shut, so they've gone to live normal lives. Well, kind of."

"Kind of? Let's *kind of* cut down on cryptic response time and have the explanation."

She rolled her eyes. "Chen's been gone from home a long time, but he and Yarvin became friends, so the elf has taken him to Oriceran."

Daniel shook his head. "And no one will find it weird that Yarvin disappeared for twenty years?"

The pixie laughed. "Hon, it's Oriceran. Weirder stuff happens all the time."

"Good point." Daniel chuckled. "What about Kevin?"

"They set up some cover story about fake amnesia and he wandered into a police station." Madge rubbed her chin. "Tim thought it'd work because he's a more recent abductee and it doesn't appear that the Fortis jerks are looking for them. They probably don't even know about them. Asses." She retrieved her magazine, sat, and opened it. "Humans can adapt. You adapted to the truth of Oriceran well enough."

Daniel couldn't argue with that. He was talking to a pixie in glasses who read a tiny magazine while sitting beside a giant holographic globe. The future had come, and it was far weirder than he'd ever dared to imagine.

Madge sighed. "We need a place for the kid. He's nice and helpful, especially for a human. I've taken a real shine to him, even if he's not a pixie or a gnome."

"We'll figure something out." Daniel shook his head. "We can't exactly raise a child in secret taskforce head-quarters."

"I don't know about that," she replied with a little too much glee. "I think we can."

Yeah, a kid kidnapped by aliens and raised by a pixie. That's...not a good idea.

Daniel chuckled and sat at the table, thankful that he didn't need to solve every problem. He was operations head, but Timothy and Nessie were better at logistics. They would find something for Jake because they had no other choice.

Too damned much information.

Daniel shook his head. He had worked through various reports flagged by Connor for additional review. His friend's part-time analyst efforts were helpful, but they only reduced a raging torrent of possible leads to a barely manageable fast-flowing river.

He looked up to comment to Madge, but her chair was empty. For some reason, he found her ability to fly around in near silence unsettling. It inevitably conjured the image of a dark pixie assassin who flitted around and slit people's throats.

Who knows what Madge did in the past?

Daniel smirked at the image of people fleeing in terror from the deep-voiced pixie.

The elevator doors opened, and Ronni hurried out followed by Big Gnome. Their eyes were wide and their faces flushed as they stared at him.

"Can I help you?" Daniel arched a brow.

The pair rushed toward him, their expressions gleeful. Ronni bounced with evident excitement, and Big Gnome gave him an enthusiastic thumb's up.

"Okay, I'll confess. I have no idea what's going on, but then again, that seems to be the standard today." He raised a brow and waited.

"The card—" Ronni began.

"We know what it is," Big Gnome finished.

They high-fived each other.

Daniel turned to face them. "I paid a crapload of money for that thing. Please don't tell me it was an alien ad for fast-food delivery."

Ronni shook her head. "No, not at all, sir. We're sure it's a storage unit, but not merely any unit. It's an alien locational database."

"Really?"

Big Gnome slapped his palm on the table. "Between our

genius and hacking the comms device, we figured it out. Competence is part of the Big Gnome brand."

Daniel chuckled and nodded.

Ronni slipped into a chair beside the agent and gestured with her hands as she spoke. "Look, we're not saying we one-hundred-percent—or even, like, fifteen percent—understand how it works. But like he said, we have interfaced it with the comms device. It definitely identifies different places on Earth."

"That's promising." Daniel's eyes glazed a little as he thought hard. "Maybe alien bases or equipment locations."

She nodded. "Maybe. Several are locations we've already flagged, but there are two that we haven't. We're still working on accessing more data, but that's a start."

Big Gnome grinned. "They are probably where they keep their ships."

"We don't even know if they have ships," Daniel pointed out.

"Of course they have ships. They are aliens." The gnome scoffed.

"Technically, *you're* an alien."

"No, I'm not. I was born in the United States."

"Okay, good point." Daniel shrugged. "So, where are these two new locations?"

Ronni tapped a few commands into her phone. Two bright flashing red dots appeared on the holographic globe which immediately zoomed in on the west coast of the United States. "The first one is in central Oregon, a small town called Clark's Pass." The globe spun and zoomed in on western China. "The other is in a desert in the Xinjiang region of China."

"We could strike at both locations." Daniel nodded. "John has his field legs back, so he and I could go to one and Daisy to the other. ASAP, too, if only because we don't know how stale this intelligence is."

"Someone should hit Oregon immediately," a voice commented from the other side of the table.

Heads swiveled in that direction. Paul sat there with a computer open in front of him. He shrugged, scratched his beard, then tapped three times on the table and muttered under his breath.

When did he get here?

Daniel nodded slowly. "And we should do that because?"

Paul looked briefly at him. "Oh, because of Thomas Bernard."

"The scientist John guarded back in the day who was doing research on the missing cities?" Daniel frowned.

"Yeah. From the little I've found and what John mentioned, the guy's research seems very similar to what you've followed up on regarding energy trails and stuff. The Baja thing wasn't a coincidence." Paul exhaled sharply. "One, two, three."

Daniel pinched the bridge of his nose. "I understand that, but what does that have to do with Oregon?"

"Oh, yes. After Big Gnome and Ronni pulled the data, I ran a deep check on the two new locations to see if anything popped." Paul looked at Ronni, who smiled at him. "It turns out the OSS relocated Bernard to Clark's Pass after the war. After that, government records state that he mysteriously disappeared, but it's too much of a coincidence. Maybe *they* didn't want anyone else to follow up on him."

Daniel considered the ramifications. Even though he couldn't mention it to his allies, from what he'd been told, the Munich gun had probably been around for decades. There was still a good chance they'd find something useful or even similar in Oregon. If the town was on the aliens' radar, that meant his team should focus on it too.

"Okay," Daniel replied. "It's been a long time, but maybe we'll get lucky and find something interesting. It sounds like a promising target. I'll grab John and some gear, and we'll fly to Oregon."

WELCOME TO CLARK'S PASS
POPULATION 504

Daniel glanced at the sign as their rental SUV cruised into the heart of the small city. He clicked on the wipers when small droplets of rain slapped the front windshield.

John's gaze swept over their surroundings. "You know, it's funny."

"What is?" Daniel hoped the OSS agent wouldn't make a seasonal pun on his name like Troy had.

"I read about how this place used to be a big logging town. That all ended for a number of reasons, and it's been dying slowly ever since." John shrugged. "We came out of the Depression and into the war, but we all believed things would be great once we won. A shiny new future awaited us. Hell, even I thought so. I'd take a few Nazis out, do my part, and settle down, and even get a normal job in some big office." He sucked in a breath. "But history isn't a rocket shooting forward, is it? No matter what we tell ourselves. Shit happens, and we have to deal with it. People lose their jobs. Their towns die. Bad men raise armies and cause trouble."

Daniel slowed as they reached the town proper. It had nothing fancy to offer, mostly one and two-story buildings. Weeds in parking lots and boards over windows marked the abandoned shops and restaurants. A few people wandered the streets in jackets, ignoring the light sprinkle of rain.

"The world keeps turning, sure," Daniel replied. "These days, we can say the worlds keep turning, but if we do our job, we can make sure that people suffer less. That's good enough to keep me going."

John grinned and nodded. "You're right, Danny boy. I'm merely being an old man again." He slapped his cheeks and shook his head. "So, do you have some doodads to identify aliens here?"

Daniel snorted. "I wish. We have some AR glasses, but I think we'll have to do this the old-fashioned way and ask around. If Paul and Ronni couldn't find much, it means there isn't much to find."

"What's our cover, or do we simply claim to be mysterious G-men?"

Daniel grinned. "Nah, here's what we're going to do."

The front desk clerk at the motel, a girl barely out of high school, eyed them with suspicion. "You guys don't look like truckers with your fancy suits and all. We mostly get truckers." She popped her gum as if to prove her point.

John glanced at Daniel.

The agent looked at the woman's nametag. "No, Stella, we're not truckers. We're researchers."

Her face scrunched up. "Researchers? Meaning what? What are you researching here? Motels?"

Daniel smiled brightly. "We're traveling around the Pacific Northwest doing background research for a documentary series on towns that experience difficult economic transitions."

Stella frowned. "Is that a fancy way of saying you're looking for old, dying logging and mill towns?"

"Old places where factories closed, too," John interjected.

She snorted. "Yeah, this place is a dump. If I had more money, I would have left for Eugene or Portland—or anywhere, really." She shrugged. "But my family's here."

Daniel nodded. "I understand. Sometimes, these documentaries can help. They can promote tourism, that sort of thing, and maybe help revitalize a place a little."

Stella studied them, suspicion returning to her eyes. "And you are documentary researchers? You look more like feds in those suits." She pointed at John. "With that hat, he looks like a mobster."

John chuckled and removed his fedora.

"I'm Daniel White." The CIA agent nodded to his partner. "And this is John Castle."

He wondered if they should have used disguises and

not only fake names, but he doubted they would run into Fortis even if they did find a lead in town. Paul and Timothy had checked into CIA activity and found no evidence that the agency had shown interest in the town in the decades since Thomas Bernard's disappearance.

Maybe a proto-Fortis made him disappear.

Stella sighed. "As cool as getting tourists might be, there's not much story to tell. The logging industry dried up, and the jobs with it. The town's been bleeding people ever since. My mom told me the residents thought there might be some big change once all that Oriceran stuff came up. People thought maybe we'd have special wood nearby they could use, but nothing." She shrugged.

John leaned forward and flashed the girl a charming smile. "Hey, doll…I mean, Stella. The thing is, sometimes it's good to have a hook, something interesting. It can be anything as long as it's something unique about your town."

The agent's clumsy language aside, he'd expressed the right idea. Daniel reminded himself that the older man had missed almost a century and had been incarcerated by the CIA after that. It was amazing that he could function at all with so many social and technological changes. Daniel wasn't sure he'd be able to do it if someone brought him almost a century forward in time.

Stella tapped her bottom lip and scrunched her nose. "Something unique?"

The men nodded.

She snapped her fingers. "Oh, I've got it. It's a great hook for your documentary. Maybe even a great hook for a new documentary. And it could be good for tourism."

The agents exchanged looks before the older man asked, "What is it?"

"There's an old haunted Victorian on the edge of the town." Stella snorted. "It's actually been haunted since the Fifties. Most people didn't believe it until Oriceran, but they do now."

"Haunted?" Daniel asked. "What happened there? Murder?"

Stella shrugged. "I don't know the details. Folks don't like to talk about it. The rumor is a guy moved in shortly after World War II. They say he was a French nuclear scientist smuggled out of Nazi Germany and that he was working on nukes for them."

John's face twitched. "What was his name?"

The girl shook her head. "I don't know."

Daniel frowned. "Why would some scientist moving into a house make it haunted?"

"Because rumors also say he wasn't really French or a nuke researcher, but some messed-up German doctor who did human experiments and stuff. He gave his research to our guys, and they agreed to let him go, but then he couldn't help himself." Stella glanced furtively around, then leaned in and lowered her voice. "He continued his research in a hidden room in the basement of that house. Twisted stuff."

Daniel nodded slowly. "Did anyone go missing around that time?"

Stella sighed and shook her head. "I know it sounds like a small-town urban legend, but no one has ever wanted to live in that house since, and it used to be nice. Years later, someone bought the property and inspected it. It was so full of radon that they decided it wasn't worth it. I've heard the government even brought some wizards in to inspect it, and they found unusual magic there."

"Could you give us the address?" Daniel asked. "We'd love to check it out. You're right. It could be a great hook."

Stella blew a gum bubble and popped it. "Sure thing, but no way in hell am I coming with you."

"Thanks, Ronni. We're going offline now." Daniel squeezed his earlobe to disabled his comms implant.

John sat on the other bed in the dingy motel room. "What'd she say?"

"She has the drone in a holding pattern over the house and has gone through the satellite images." Daniel exhaled slowly. "They show unusual thermal traces and energy readings of different types."

John hopped up and dusted his hands. "So, we have ourselves a haunted house?"

Daniel shook his head. "Not necessarily. There aren't any easy technological ways to detect magic."

The other man nodded toward the door. "But you heard what doll-face said about the wizards being brought in?"

"Nope. Ronni checked. There are no PDA records associated with this place, and no public inspection results or anything similar. If wizards did come in, they did it under the radar." Daniel shrugged. "That said, the place might very well be haunted, or at least inhabited by a magical creature."

John rubbed his neck. "Ghosts weren't a thing the OSS made me deal with back in the day. Does the CIA have official ghost-catching doodads now?"

The younger agent shook his head. "That's more a PDA thing, and ghosts can manifest as different kinds of phenomenon. Let's grab our gear and hit it tonight. It's better to do this when it's dark and without curious witnesses."

His partner laughed. "Yeah, of course, we'll investigate the haunted house in the middle of the night. Too bad we didn't bring our magic elf dame with us."

CHAPTER ELEVEN

The two agents stepped cautiously out of the SUV.
Both wore AR glasses and wrist flashlights, along
with tactical belts filled with everything from EMP disks
to salt. John suggested the latter with a vague statement
that ghosts possibly couldn't cross salt barriers. Daniel
hadn't heard of that but decided it wouldn't hurt to try it if
nothing else worked.

Even though the glasses provided a good night-vision
mode, the flashlights would offer better plausible denia-
bility if locals arrived and demanded to know what they
were doing.

Nature had long since reclaimed what passed for the
lawn. Shrubs and tall grasses now surrounded the dilapi-
dated building. Much of the roof had already caved in, and
branches from nearby trees reached over it like angry,
protective nature spirits. The decaying remains of the
front door, riddled with holes from hungry insects and
rodents, lay on the porch. Most of the windows were

cracked or broken as if someone had used them for target practice.

Daniel's flashlight cut through the darkness. No ghosts and no murderous rabid elves rushed to meet them. Thick cobwebs lined the foyer above piles of debris and rat droppings. He could even hear a few squeaks.

He glanced at John. "You don't have a problem with rats, do you?"

The other man snorted. "Rats can't shoot you."

Daniel shrugged. "A Willen probably could."

"What's a Willen?"

The younger man stepped into the house and swept his flashlight to either side. "Think of a rat that's as intelligent as a human, the size of a small dog, and walks on two legs."

John scrubbed a hand over his face. "I knew a lot more about this hocus pocus than the average Joe even back then, and I still can't believe all the stuff you guys deal with now."

"Like ghosts?" Daniel grinned.

"I understand dead guys. They are old-school." John tapped the side of his AR glasses. "How do I change the specs to see heat?" He pulled them off and shook them a few times. "Damn magic glasses."

His partner took them and pointed at a notch on the frame. "It's tech, not magic. They can take voice commands, too, but for now, work with the preprogrammed modes. A quick tap near the top will give you thermal vision, and another will restore normal vision. You can cycle through other spectra by tapping on the bottom."

John slipped them on and tapped the frame. "I don't know whether the magic or the tech is harder to adjust to.

All this science seems like Buck Rogers to me, and he never appealed to me. Somehow, elves doing magic makes sense, but computers and satellites? That's some crazy stuff."

They moved into the living room which was in much the same shape as the foyer. No furniture remained, and numerous holes gouged the walls. The sharp scent of animal urine soured the air. A sudden movement in the corner revealed several scurrying rats.

Most men would have recoiled, but they'd both seen far worse.

The stairs leading to the second floor were a death trap. Rope would be needed if they wanted to reach the top floor.

"I grew up with the internet and computers," Daniel continued in the silence. "It's second-nature to me. Even as a kid, I heard how we were one step away from curing diseases with genetic engineering and had space telescopes that could see billions of light-years away, so science and technology were my normal. Magic and that kind of thing seemed like silly kid's stuff or superstition." He shrugged. "Then Oriceran happened. It doesn't matter that some people like you knew the truth. Most of us didn't."

"And now these Martians, too." John chuckled.

"They probably aren't Martians."

John grinned. "Give an old man his Martians. You know what I don't get, though?"

Daniel looked his way. "What?"

"Why don't you have more robots? You have stuff we couldn't think of back then but few metal men."

"We have some. There are plenty of robots in factories, for example."

John shrugged. "Yeah, but with all the fancy tech, I figured the Army would be nothing but metal men by now."

Daniel chuckled. "It sounds good in theory, but it's more difficult in practice. Hackers are too damned good, and that makes it hard for the military and police to use autonomous weapons. We've had some embarrassing and lethal mistakes made with autonomous drones and tanks." Daniel blew out a breath and shook his head. "But the truth is that the chaos of Oriceran and magic returning messed everything up for a while. In a sense, it all froze, and we're only now moving forward. Magic still seems easier to a lot of people, even if the CIA's afraid of it."

"They had all this time to get used to it, but they are still trying to figure it out." John grinned. "Some things never change, do they? The brass screws things up and keeps the useful weapons from us grunts on the ground."

"True enough." Daniel snorted.

They headed into another rotting room across the hall. A half-decayed possum lay in the corner.

"How did you end up in OSS?" Daniel asked. "I'm the guy they sent to grab you, but I never knew that much about your background."

John crouched and examined the floor. "I was a paratrooper in the Army and saw a little action in Africa." He shrugged. "One day, some suits showed up. They liked my record and said I did well on some personality tests. I barely even remembered taking the tests. They pulled the same move as you and gave me a speech about being another grunt or fighting the war in a new way and saving the world. Next thing I knew, I was a spook running around and worrying about not only the Germans but magic as well. What about you? I heard you were a Marine?"

"Yeah, in signals intelligence. I was well-trained but probably didn't see the kind of action you did. The CIA was already sniffing around me before I got out." Daniel shrugged. "My parents were tomb raiders. They spent their lives looking for magical artifacts, so I was primed for that kind of thing."

John's gaze remained fixed on the floor, and a frown spread across his face. "I heard your parents disappeared."

"Yeah." Daniel sighed. "With everything I've seen now, I realize they might have crossed paths with aliens but can't be sure. I want to believe they're still alive, but that might simply be wishful thinking."

The other agent stood and shook his head. "It's still a possibility. From what I found out, my parents never knew what really happened to me. They were told I was still in the Army and went MIA during D-Day. Now, they're six feet under, and I never got to say goodbye."

The silence stretched between them as they reflected upon their losses.

John cleared his throat and pointed to the floor. "I'm not sure, but I think I see something."

Grateful to refocus on the mission, Daniel switched to thermal mode. A faint heat signature glowed beneath the current room and a bright, fluctuating signature a little further out—a group of rats from what he could tell. He switched to normal vision and headed into the hall toward the door to the basement stairs. "Can you recall anything else about Thomas Bernard you think might be helpful?"

John tapped his glasses several times and muttered. He finally restored them to normal mode and followed. "I know very little about his research. The OSS was worried the Nazis might be on the verge of acquiring some sort of magical 'city-killer,' which is why they had me guarding him. From what Bernard told me, historical records exist regarding certain mythical cities that simply disappeared. Poof. One day they were there, and the next day, they had vanished. Of course, these were simply stories." He shook his head. "But even if they weren't, it doesn't matter. While I was rotting in Germany, our boys made the A-bomb. Talk about a city killer."

The basement door fell off its hinges at Daniel's touch, and the soggy, cracked wood thudded to the floor. He kicked it out of the way. "My parents were in Belize when they disappeared. A village disappeared there, too. It wasn't a nuke, and it doesn't seem to be magic. That's why I can't help but think it has something to do with aliens."

"I'm willing to believe anything nowadays." John directed his flashlight down the stairs. He sighed with relief. "At least they're concrete. I didn't look forward to risking my neck down half-eaten wooden steps."

Daniel nodded and started down. The talk of his parents reminded him of the *Codex of the Sky Gods*. He'd been angry with Timothy for keeping secrets, but he kept enough of his own. It was obvious now that he wouldn't solve the mystery of his parents without help and holding back a useful resource from the rest of the team was counterproductive.

They have the tech, and Big Gnome and Ronni even figured

out how to use the location card. If I bring the Codex to the brownstone, maybe we can all figure the truth out together.

Daniel's flashlight swept the stairs. More rats scurried away from the light. He'd considered switching to night-vision mode, locals be damned, but preferred the idea of the pests fleeing before he stepped into a writhing mass of disease.

He pulled a small sensor wand from his jacket pocket. "Thanks, Nessie." He peered at the readout on the side. "Do you know what I'm *not* detecting?"

John shook his head.

"Any significant radiation levels. We have very faint thermal signatures but no radiation." Daniel nodded. "I think there's something here, but it's not radon."

Their footsteps echoed in the basement above the scurrying sounds of small rodents. The deeper they descended, the stronger the nauseating stench grew. The rats ran past them and upstairs.

Daniel grimaced and slipped the sensor wand back in his jacket. "The glamorous life of a secret agent."

John barked a laugh. The loud noise sent the remaining rats scarpering past their feet. "I hear you, Danny boy. I hear you."

Their flashlights illuminated cracked and weathered concrete, small pools of water along one wall, and dirt infiltrating along the side of another.

Daniel turned toward the opposite wall. They'd both noticed a small thermal signature that indicated something that appeared to be behind the concrete. He tapped the frame of his glasses. At this angle, he could make out two faint orange-red signatures, larger than rats and opposite each other, but above the ceiling. There was also another faint signature in the wall close to where they stood.

He deactivated thermal mode, walked over, and knocked on the wall. The thump sounded more hollow than solid, and he grinned over his shoulder at John. "I think we have a hidden room here and maybe some artifacts hidden in the ceiling."

John nodded. "How do we get inside?"

Daniel pulled a glove on and ran his hand over the wall near where he'd seen the thermal trace. He felt a faint dip and pressed gently. Something clicked, and a loud hum filled the room. The agents backed up and frowned.

A soft red light illuminated the basement with no apparent source. Both men drew their guns at the same time. With a loud groan, a slab of concrete folded in the back wall to reveal another large chamber.

Dust and cobwebs covered several tables in the center of the room. Large metal shelves filled with beakers, flasks, and glass pipettes lined the walls. Sealed clear jars containing various liquids, their true colors disguised by the red light, stood on other shelves beside various mechanical parts and metals bits. Broken glass littered the floor, and numerous small indentations and holes covered the walls.

"Shit," Daniel muttered as his gaze swept to the corner.

A skeleton in rotting clothes lay there, several of its ribs broken inward. A few dark stains were visible on what remained of the scraps of the skeleton's shirt and pants.

John sighed. "I think we found our missing Thomas Bernard."

"Yeah." Daniel looked around. "And some sort of hidden

lab. There's still the ceiling, though. Maybe he hid something up there before he died."

A scraping noise sounded overhead, followed quickly by another.

Daniel frowned. "Do you hear that?"

John frowned and aimed his pistol toward the concrete ceiling.

Two small slabs in opposite corners retracted. Daniel covered one corner with his gun and John the other.

Four pointed, dull metal legs appeared from the darkness of the retracted slab and speared the nearby wall, knocking some concrete loose. A second later, four more legs emerged, along with a squat cylindrical body formed by twisted coils of metal. A glowing blue sphere sat in the center.

"What the hell?" John muttered as more of the creatures emerged. "Robot spiders?"

Daniel narrowed his eyes. "I think we know what killed Thomas, assuming that's his body."

The metal creatures skittered along the wall, their pointed legs ripping new holes to hold them in place.

Daniel selected a target and held his breath as he waited for the inevitable attack. The arachnids dropped from the wall and landed on tables. In seconds, they charged the men.

Muzzle flashes lit up the small room and bullets struck home, denting the bodies. John's fifth bullet pierced one and slammed into the blue sphere. The creature crumpled and slid off a table.

Daniel's target leapt at him and he dodged to the side, still firing. A metal leg snagged and tore a strap on his vest, but the close attack enabled him to put a bullet through the blue heart. It crashed to the ground, and the clang echoed loudly. The red light disappeared. The flashlights' beams sliced through the darkness once again.

The CIA agent released a breath and reloaded. He winced at a sudden stinging sensation on his chest. The spider hadn't only torn his vest but had ripped through the shirt and into his skin.

"You okay?" John asked.

"It's a scratch." Daniel pointed his weapon at holes in the ceiling, his wound now throbbing. John did the same. They stood there for about a minute before lowering their guns.

"Do you think our guy was assassinated?" John asked, holstering his pistol.

Daniel shook his head as he retrieved a self-adhering analgesic bandage and slapped it on his wound. The pain immediately receded. "Those retracting slabs were built into this place. Whatever those things were, I think they are part of the security." He snorted. "Yeah, this is why I don't trust robots. You can't even trust metal spiders. Let's get a bone fragment for DNA analysis and look around for anything else."

John blew the dust from a nearby table and picked up a small leather-bound book. "Like this?"

"Yes. That works." Daniel took the book. He opened it to the first page and frowned. After a few seconds, he realized it was in French. Thankfully, his French was far better than his Spanish. He read a few lines. "This is Thomas Bernard's journal."

John nodded. "Let's spend a few minutes looking for

more, then get the hell out of here before some metal python shows up."

Daniel snorted. "Good plan."

Under the harsh light of the motel lamps, Daniel stared at the journal's yellowed pages. They'd found nothing else useful in the hidden lab. He suspected some of the liquids or parts might be magical, but he was far less interested in magic than what the journal might reveal.

His partner leaned over his shoulder. "How's it going?"

"Slowly. A lot of shorthand, that kind of thing, but I can generally follow it."

John stepped back and leaned against the wall. "I never learned French. Only German."

Daniel shook his head. "We're damned lucky to have found this. If it weren't in that sealed lab, it would probably have become lining in some shit-filled rat bed. It's not all that exciting so far, though. Mostly, it's how much he hated being stuck in rural America, and how all the locals were ignorant fools with no sense of proper cooking, according to him."

John snorted. "A stuck-up Frenchman wasn't exactly exotic, even back in my day. Mind you, I met some solid Frenchies with the Maquis back during the war."

The CIA agent chuckled involuntarily. He narrowed his eyes and murmured under his breath as he translated the next page.

"What?" John asked.

"There are a few more entries after this, but let me

roughly translate it for you. 'I've grown bored with my research. The Americans have forced me into exile, and I will never be able to pursue the lost cities, so I've turned to another path. The encounter with the wizard in Prague already showed me I had greater potential, but I let the Americans worry me with their petty concerns over the Germans.

'The wizard was a fool. The strength of humanity is in our minds and our technology, this new age of wonder. We should mix technology and magic to gain the strength of both, but the foolish guardians, those damnable Silver Griffins, retard our progress to keep their conspiracy of silence about Oriceran.

'But I will not be stopped. I will prove the superiority of my approach with my magiomechano spiders. Yes, I have some difficulty with threat assessment, but I'm confident I can overcome it. There have been some strangers in town lately with strange accents. I do wonder if some old Germans have come to settle their scores with me. I don't worry. My spiders will protect me.'"

Daniel frowned. "Was he some sort of latent wizard? Did you know?"

John shook his head. "Nope. As far as anyone told me, he was nothing but a researcher. Hey, are those Silver Griffin bastards still around? The ones I dealt with were a damned smug bunch of people trying to dictate who knew about magic."

"They're not really a thing anymore." The agent chuckled. "They met a bad end. Now, smug bastards like us get to decide who knows about aliens." He sighed. "This proves there was no grand conspiracy, though, merely a mad scientist who had a lab accident."

John shrugged. "What about the Germans he mentioned?"

"His rib cage was caved in. I think they would have simply shot him. Even if Germans were looking for him, they obviously never found that lab." Daniel turned a page, and his eyes widened. "What the fuck?"

John hurried over. "What is it?"

Daniel pointed to the page. Alien glyphs filled one side with carefully detailed notes to the right. He held up a finger, indicating to John to wait while he read through the entries.

"This was a few days after the note about the spiders. He wanted to detail the most important things he'd discovered about the lost city legends and some work he'd done on translating what he called the 'Language of the Lemurians.'"

John frowned. "Lemurians?"

Daniel scratched his cheek. "There was a theory back in the nineteenth century about a lost continent in either the Indian or Pacific Oceans."

"You mean like Atlantis?"

"Yeah, the same idea of a vanished powerful ancient civilization, only with a different location and culture." Daniel flipped the page and read further. "Bernard was convinced the lost cities had something to do with the Lemurians. He didn't seem to realize they were aliens." Daniel blinked. "Huh. I think he's translated some glyphs we haven't. Give me a few minutes."

He flipped through more pages, read the notes, and soaked in the new knowledge before he shook his head.

"No go?" John asked.

Daniel looked at him, bemused. "This isn't the Rosetta Stone, but the glyph information will still help our translation efforts. There's nothing else about the lost city here. He mentions American agents taking most of his notes on that." He ground his teeth. "Damn it. We were so fucking close to a breakthrough."

John patted him on the shoulder. "Hey, if we crack the language, maybe we won't need old books from dead guys."

"You're right." Daniel closed the journal and took a deep breath. "We're closer now. We have the communication device, more information on the glyphs, and decent proof that these lost city legends are connected with the aliens. Perhaps they stole whole cities in the past but now stick to rural villages and the occasional person. We need to get this information back to the brownstone."

He closed the journal and the disappointment faded as his heart rate kicked up in excitement. If his team could translate the symbols, they might be able to understand the meaning of some of the diagrams in the *Codex of the Sky Gods.*

I'm closer than I've ever been.

CHAPTER TWELVE

The next afternoon, Daniel sat opposite Timothy in his brownstone office.

His mentor wasn't frowning, and his expression even approached a smile. "The new glyph information will definitely be useful." His pseudo-smile disappeared. "Daisy investigated the other site. She detected unusual energy readings there, but that was it. At least you found something."

Daniel rubbed his forehead. "The only thing I don't understand is why the aliens even had that location marked. There was no alien tech there, only Thomas Bernard. It looked like his own spiders killed him, but they were a combination of magic and old human technology. And the journal was still there as well."

Timothy shrugged. "They might have looked for him. If the lost city legends are related to the aliens, he might have known too much and they wanted to shut him up. They probably popped by, but by the time they'd tracked him down he was already dead, so they didn't care."

"That would explain his mention of the Germans. It must have been aliens."

Ronni ran through the open doorway, her hand over her chest as she took rapid breaths.

Daniel craned his head around to stare at her.

She blinked several times. "Oh, sorry, um...I can come back."

Timothy arched a brow. "Just spit it out, Ronni."

She chuckled nervously. "Oh, well, Paul, Big Gnome, and I have worked on accessing more information from that data card. That's what we call it, by the way. We were able to identify three new points. One of them is the Baja California site where Daniel and Daisy found those bodies. Another is in Belize and near a village that allegedly disappeared there."

Daniel's heart pounded.

That proves it. Damn it. The aliens did have something to do with my parents' disappearance.

"And the third?" he managed to ask without his voice shaking.

"Middle of nowhere Australia," Ronni replied. "We saw nothing unusual on the satellites, and it doesn't have any incidents associated with it like Belize has."

Daniel frowned and looked at Timothy. "We should check out the Australia site immediately."

The older man closed his eyes, took a deep breath, and released it slowly. "No."

"No?" Daniel leapt from his chair, fighting to keep the anger and suspicion off his face. Timothy already had fragments of his father's journal and knew his disappearance had something to do with the aliens, but he'd kept it to himself. Was he trying to hide the truth now?

"Look, Daniel, we can't make any immediate moves. I came across some disturbing information at the agency. I'm ninety percent convinced Fortis is watching you now. It's not only about Troy Williams being partnered with you but also what happened in Paraguay." Timothy shrugged.

Daniel frowned. "Paraguay? Lowry?"

Ronni cleared her throat. "Didn't Paul tell you, sir?"

He shook his head. "Tell me what?"

"He dug around, and he says he's sure Lowry and the other agents are Fortis."

Daniel scrubbed his hand with his face. "Why don't they simply eliminate me, then?" he all but shouted.

Ronni winced and stepped back.

Timothy shrugged. "Like I told you before, they might be evaluating you as both a risk or a potential recruit. I'm merely saying we should wait, especially after we sent you off to Oregon on a rogue mission. We need to be more careful."

"Fine." Daniel adjusted his tie and forced a smile on his face. "I'll wait. If we're done here, then, I have to make an appearance. That should make Fortis worry less if they are watching me."

Timothy lowered his brows but nodded.

Daniel walked past Ronni. He stopped at the door and looked over his shoulder. "If you had more samples of the alien writing, do you think you'd have a better shot at decoding some of it?"

"Of course." Ronni shrugged. "The stuff in the journal is a good start, but every little bit helps."

"Thanks."

He left the office, his thoughts returning to the *Codex of the Sky Gods*. As much as he wanted to hand it over, his confrontation with Timothy would need to come first. Even if his mentor's excuses sounded reasonable, that didn't alter the fact that he'd withheld information.

This isn't over. I'm close to my parents now, and I won't let anyone block me.

Daniel maneuvered past several tables filled with crockpots, food-laden trays, and stuffed baskets containing everything from fruit to fried chicken. The late afternoon sun baked down on them, but the light breeze refreshed everyone present.

He smiled with real pleasure as he sat in the metal folding chair. Their long picnic table, one of a dozen set up in two rows, was covered with a red checkerboard tablecloth.

Tommy and his grandfather, Peter, flanked him on either side with Mrs. Carmichael, Simon, and Jeanine across from them. Mrs. Carmichael's event contribution included planning and blessing everyone with her wonderfully elaborate broad-brimmed silk hat festooned with flowers. Simon had provided a variety of bagels. The centerpieces of each table—seasonal flowers—were courtesy of Jeanine and her father.

"You work too hard, Daniel," Mrs. Carmichael admonished him after a bite of fried chicken. "You're always traveling. If my Mr. Carmichael, God rest his soul, had traveled as much as you as a young man, we would never have even met."

Tommy nodded his agreement. "Yeah, Daniel. You're supposed to run the shop, but instead, you're always off buying or looking for stuff."

Peter chuckled as he sipped on a cup of Fresca with ice.

Daniel shrugged and offered the elderly woman a disarming smile. "But travel's interesting. Maybe I'll meet someone on one of those trips."

Simon shook his head. "I've tried the long-distance thing. It does not work, let me tell you that."

Jeanine smiled at him, her cheeks coloring. "Yeah, it's best to always look for local relationships."

The agent took a bite from a piece of chicken to hide his grin. Jeanine was cute enough, but she wasn't his type, and nor would she fit in his world. Despite what Troy said about lying to people, Daniel rejected the idea of continually misleading someone in a relationship. He'd decided that his woman, if and when he found her, would have to be part of his secret world.

Like Daisy.

Where the hell did that come from?

Daisy was beautiful, intelligent, strong, and magical—literally. But he also worked with her and dating someone in the workplace, even one as unusual as his, could lead to complications. What would happen if they had a bad breakup? Finding skilled operatives whom he could trust for his rogue alien-hunting group wasn't simply a matter of visiting an employment website.

Daniel swallowed another bite of chicken. "I'm glad everyone's so concerned about my love life."

They all laughed, though Jeanine's face turned scarlet.

Simon shook his head. "Setting the future Mrs. Winters aside, I'm merely happy we could even have this block party."

Peter frowned. "What are you talking about?"

The shop owner pointed his thumb at Jeanine. "Thugs showing up at the corner grocery or trying to mug Jeanine and her dad. For a while there, I was worried this neighborhood would go to hell."

Jeanine shuddered. "It was scary. I don't know what I would have done if Daniel and his military buddies hadn't been there."

He shrugged. "We only did what anyone would have done."

Mrs. Carmichael clucked her tongue. "I agree with Simon. Those no-good boys are gone now, but they were bold. Even if most of them ran off because they had trouble with other bad men, that doesn't change the fact that Daniel also saw to that fool who made a scene at the grocery store." She nodded. "Um-hmm."

Tommy grinned at him. "You're so badass."

"I'm a shop owner, Tommy."

"A badass shop owner."

Peter snickered under his breath.

"Don't you start, too, Pops." Daniel shot him a mock glare.

The old man grinned, leaned back, and hooked his thumbs in his pockets. "There's nothing wrong with your neighbors appreciating what you do, Daniel."

Mrs. Carmichael nodded. "Exactly. I think that's why we like to think of you as the mayor. I know you're busy running your granddad's old shop and all, but you're always there when we need it, and we appreciate it."

A warm smile filled Daniel's face. When he crawled through rat-infested ruins or snuck into a mobster's house to steal a dangerous artifact, he could lose sight of what the CIA and the Codex group meant. The people at the table and the dozens at the other tables didn't care about alien conspiracies or geopolitics. They wanted nothing more than to live their lives in peace.

He could protect them from all the horrors that lurked in the shadows.

We can do it, John. We can do it, Troy. We can protect this world and these people as long as we're all on the same page.

Jake hurried, uncloaked, down the stairs to the basement of Rooney's Antiquities and Oddities. The cameras in the shop were temporarily disabled, but he didn't care if Daniel discovered the truth later. By then, the transformation guns would be gone. When Jake heard the CIA agent mention a block party as he left the brownstone, he realized he'd been handed the opportunity to recover the guns.

This time he was far more prepared. He ran his thumb along the edge of his resonator. The device whined, and the pitch grew sharper until he could no longer hear it. A low hum followed, and a basement wall slid down to reveal the sealed metal door of the vault.

He ignored the keypad and DNA scanner and retrieved a thin silver square barely the size of his currently child-sized thumb. He pressed the square against the keypad and waited. A few seconds later, the bolts released with a loud thud. He recovered the square and turned the wheel on the front of the door, his temporarily weaker muscles straining. The door finally opened.

Jake smiled. He hadn't worried about gaining entry. The security might be impressive for humans, but his people's technology was far more advanced. He'd merely needed the time to prepare and the opportunity.

He stepped inside and saw the transformation guns within seconds. The alien hurried forward and yanked two tiny, glossy, black pyramid-shaped devices from his pocket. With a quick push against the first gun, the locational transponder adhered to the metal.

A faint buzz followed, and an inky pool appeared below the weapon. The gun shadowed and broke into smaller chunks which seemed to melt into the darkness. The whole process was over in seconds, and the gun teleported safely.

Jake grinned. For all their caution, this had been far easier than he'd anticipated. He moved to the next one and stopped. His stomach twisted. The control rod lay loose on the shelf.

He ran a scanner probe over the rod, and the results winked into existence above the device on a virtual holographic screen.

"No, no, no."

The control rod was fake; just a human-made replica.

"What game are you playing, Daniel?" Jake slammed his fist against the shelf, rattling the contents.

He affixed another transponder to the weapon and watched it disappear into a teleportation vortex.

Jake took several deep breaths. He'd recovered their

technology, but the human had been smart enough to produce a fake rod. The actual part could be in some secret lab and under examination by human scientists.

The primary mission had been accomplished, but he wouldn't bother to ask for permission for the next part. Daniel knew where the real control rod was, and Jake would force that information out of him. The safety of his people was at stake.

The alien yanked a cell phone from his pocket and dialed the number of Daniel's brownstone phone.

"Hello?" the agent answered, suspicion coloring his voice.

"This is Jake. Come to the vault in your shop right away. Bring no one else, or there will be trouble. If you think you can defeat me, let me make it clear that I've already taken the guns."

He hung up and scoffed. He'd been forced into a child's body for far too long.

<hr>

The CIA agent hurried down the street. He'd made a few quick apologies to everyone and simply said he'd be back in a moment. When Tommy suggested he really needed to go to the bathroom, Daniel didn't bother to disabuse anyone of the notion. A lie about needing to check on the shop would involve both Tommy and his grandfather, and the last thing he needed was innocent people caught in the crossfire.

He could already see the suspicion in his grandfather's

eyes. Leaving so abruptly after a phone call wasn't exactly subtle.

Jake? It sounded like his voice but not his words. This is some sort of trap. Fortis? But they don't know about the kid.

Daniel threw the door to the shop open and rushed toward the back room and the basement stairs. He drew a small pistol concealed in his ankle holster. A suit wasn't good block-party wear, but the lack of it made it harder to hide a weapon.

He reached the bottom of the stairs and stopped.

Jake stood in the doorway of the vault, his arms folded and a scowl on his face. "Go ahead. Try to shoot me if you want to. Your primitive weapon can't penetrate my personal shield."

The agent kept the gun pointed at the boy for several seconds before he tossed it on a nearby table. "If you were simply going to kill me, you would have already. Right, Jake? Or whoever the hell you really are."

The boy stepped forward. "You know exactly who I am. You took something that didn't belong to you. Two things that didn't belong to you."

They locked eyes, both angry statues for a moment.

"You basically left nukes around for anyone to find," Daniel replied finally. "People died because of your mistakes. They died horribly."

The boy's face twitched for a second. "That…wasn't our intent. Still, you can't make accusations, Daniel. You've hoarded dangerous weapons, and you've stolen one of the control rods." He narrowed his eyes. "I heard what you've said at the brownstone, but that doesn't mean I believe it.

After all, you had those guns hidden here. They don't even know about them, do they?"

Daniel snorted. "So what? Do you think I'm with Fortis?"

"No, I think your kind find justification for all sorts of viciousness." Jake sneered. "If you didn't, maybe we wouldn't need the transformation guns."

Transformation guns? That is a little catchier that molecular rearrangement guns.

Daniel absorbed the information and exhaled a long, slow breath. "If I'm such a ruthless asshole, then why did I bother to help your people? You're the ones hiding in fake human bodies and snatching people from their friends and families." He pointed at Jake. "What gives you the right?"

He gritted his teeth. He wanted to demand why they'd taken his parents.

"We have our reasons," Jake replied flatly. "If you're not our enemy, then give me the control rod."

Daniel had no desire to tell Jake he had no idea where it was. His grandfather hadn't given him specifics on the elf contact who had hired him to find the gun and then taken the rod.

"Maybe we can work out a deal," he replied. "I've done this before with your people. I helped Matteas and Linda."

Jake snorted. "Temporary alliances are just that, human —temporary. I don't trust you. You're a spy. You're trained to lie, cheat, and kill the enemies of your country."

Daniel shook his head. "I try to protect freedom and defend innocent people from the darkness they don't even know is around them."

"Pretty words, but just words."

Jake reached into his pocket. Daniel narrowed his eyes and prepared to dodge.

"Tell the others what you want, Daniel," the alien muttered. "I won't give up, and I *will* get that control rod."

The room darkened, and a pool of impenetrable darkness formed on the floor. The boy stared at the agent as his form faded until only a thick shadow remained. It flowed, piece by piece, into the blackness below him before the pool vanished and the room brightened.

Daniel released a pent breath. "Well, *that's* fucking great."

CHAPTER THIRTEEN

From behind the front counter of Rooney's Antiquities and Oddities, Peter watched a woman in the loud floral-print dress step into the shop with a determined expression on her face. She didn't even look his way as she disappeared among the shelves, her head darting this way and that.

He needed a distraction. Daniel had told him about the alien breaking into the vault and reclaiming the guns. Even though on one level, Peter was happy that the dangerous weapons were no longer there, the idea that some alien looking like a child had strolled in and beat the vault's security pushed his heartburn to uncomfortable levels.

The old man grabbed the remaining half of a cinnamon Pop-Tart from under the counter and took a bite. Tommy had him addicted to the things. They weren't Fresca, but few things could measure up to his favorite drink. After a few more bites, he replaced the treat and decided it might be a good idea to have Tommy work part-time at the store. The boy could use a little more structure, and Daniel's real job and new alien side job had kept him away from the store more often in recent weeks.

The woman squatted near a back rack, ran her fingers along the shelf, and mumbled to herself.

"Do you need any help, miss?" Peter called.

"No, no. No, help. I'll find it myself. I have to feel it—you know, the sacred aura."

Peter furrowed his brow. "Sacred aura?"

The woman stood quickly and leaned around the shelf to look at him. "I don't mean to alarm you, but I'm fairly certain that I've traced the Holy Grail to this place."

He stared at her, waiting for her laugh, but her expression remained serious.

"The Holy Grail?" Peter shook his head. "These are all minor artifacts, ma'am. I can assure you, we might have a few medium artifacts but nothing like that."

She shook her head, her long, unruly dark hair dancing. "No. You don't understand. It's disguised, but I'll find it and I'll buy it. I must have the Holy Grail!"

Peter rubbed the back of his neck. "What makes you think I would sell it to you even if you could find it?"

The woman smiled. "You don't believe it. So, you'll sell me whatever I find for far less than it's worth, even if it *is* the Holy Grail."

Peter shrugged. "I can't argue with you there." He pointed to a shelf in the back. "Lot of cups and bowls over there if you want to check for sacred auras."

She shook her head and gave him a pitying look. "Oh, you poor, deluded man. You think it'd actually be disguised as a cup or bowl? That's the mistake most amateurs make."

Peter chuckled. "Honestly, I wouldn't know. I haven't run into a lot of Holy Grails before."

The woman moved in the opposite direction and stopped at a shelf holding a mixture of statuettes and figurines along with a few old action figures and Lego mini-figures. She rubbed her chin and nodded to herself as if satisfied.

Peter shook his head. It wasn't the first time he had encountered someone with a creative view of what was sold in the shop. Occasionally, a powerful artifact did slip through, but he sincerely doubted they'd accidentally found the Holy Grail or that it was disguised as a figurine or action figure.

The customer selected a small diorama of dogs playing poker and her eyes widened. "Amazing." She almost sprinted toward the counter.

Peter threw up a hand. "Slow down there. You break it, you buy it."

She skidded to a stop and held the diorama out in the palms of her hands. "I'll be honest and admit this is the Holy Grail in disguise."

He pointed to it. "And I'll be honest and tell you that's not the case. That's the one hundred-and-twenty-fifth-anniversary diorama celebrating the first *Poker Game* oil painting commissioned by the Brown and Bigelow company in 1894 for cigar advertisements. I don't under-stand the ins and outs of it, but a gnome told me there was some sort of resonant power in a few these things. It has to do with collective will or something like that because a wizard worked on the project. Anyway, it has really minor magic power. If you rub the different dogs' heads, you'll smell different cigars. That's it."

The woman narrowed her eyes and inspected the diorama carefully. She rubbed a dog's head and a burnt coffee scent filled the air. Scowling, she rubbed another head. This time the strong smell of cedar emanated.

She clapped. "How delightful. So it's both the Holy Grail and aromatherapy." She smiled and set the diorama down on the counter. "I'll take it."

Peter shrugged. He wouldn't turn money away. "And how would you like to pay today?"

The woman slapped gold coin on the counter. "It's an ounce."

The old man used a magnifying glass to peer at the coin, which glowed.

"What's that?" the woman asked.

"You're not the first person to come here and want to barter with something other than normal currency," Peter explained. "This little artifact can tell if something's real gold."

She frowned down at her coin. "They assured me they weren't cheating me."

Peter smiled. "Don't worry. It's real." He searched for the price of gold using his phone and frowned. "The diorama is only worth about half that, and I don't have that much change in the register."

"I said you wouldn't believe it was the Grail."

"Even if it is the Grail, I can't charge much more than I have and still sleep at night." Peter shrugged.

The woman pursed her lips and nodded. "Any recommendations for other artifacts? You wouldn't happen to have any disguised pieces of the True Cross in here, would you?"

Peter shook his head. "No, but if you like things that smell nice, I have plenty of magic candles and incense."

The woman nodded quickly. "Fine. Give me enough of those to make up the difference."

"Do you want something floral, or are you looking for something earthier?"

Daniel took a deep breath as Nessie and Timothy sat near him at the operations room table. He'd sent them both a message asking to talk to them as soon as possible and for them to check on Jake. They'd been dismissive at first, but Malcolm had checked and found the boy was gone. The agent insisted he'd explain everything in person. He didn't want to take any chances.

The early evening meeting had already started badly for Timothy who now squeezed the life out of his poor stress ball. "Where the hell is the boy, Daniel?"

Nessie folded her hands in front of her but said nothing. Her eyes reflected more than a little disappointment.

"He wasn't a kid, at least not a human kid," Daniel explained. "He admitted being an alien to me, and I don't think he's a child even by their standards. The Jake we know was simply a human bioidentical body. He had advanced tech, language, and planning, like he was alien CIA."

Timothy's face twitched. "Come again?"

Daniel shrugged. "He was an alien spy and also had

teleportation technology. I don't know if he used a holo-gram or some kind of cloaking shield when he left this building, but Madge mentioned he slept an excessive amount. I suspect he pretended to take a nap, disrupted our cameras with alien tech, and teleported into my neigh-borhood to spy on me."

Timothy and Nessie exchanged looks and waited for Daniel to continue.

He chuckled. "Aren't you going to ask?"

"Fine. Why would he feel the need to spy on you in particular?" His mentor frowned.

"Because he wasn't here to infiltrate our group or the CIA." Daniel took a breath and exhaled slowly. "He came to recover particular pieces of lost alien technology."

"The communicator and the database?" Nessie asked.

Daniel shook his head. "Two missing alien weapons, molecular rearrangement guns."

"And why would he watch you for those? You didn't find anything like that on your missions."

"That's...where you're wrong."

Nessie pursed her lips and narrowed her eyes. "Do you care to elaborate on that?"

Timothy could have turned coal into diamonds with the way he now squeezed his stress ball.

"Before I even knew about this group, I had one of the weapons," Daniel explained. "I acquired it in Munich on a side job."

"A side job collecting alien artifacts?" Timothy snorted. "Are you kidding me? And this somehow didn't make it to the CIA—or later, even us?"

Daniel shrugged. "After seeing how powerful one of

those weapons was, I decided the best thing to do was to lock it up so no one could ever be tempted to use it."

Timothy groaned and leaned back. He ran both his hands over his bald head in clear exasperation. "I can't fucking believe this. I can't believe you."

Nessie sighed. "But you mentioned two guns, Daniel."

He nodded. "I found another one in Michigan. I merely didn't report it."

"But you were already working for us, then. I can understand not wanting to release the first gun but why conceal the second?"

"I felt the same way about the second gun, and I wasn't sure I could trust even you yet."

Timothy slammed his fist on the table. "How the hell could you do this? We have to worry about Fortis, and now you betray us by keeping secrets and alien tech?"

Nessie sighed and shook her head.

Daniel pushed angrily to his feet and pointed at his mentor. "Don't feed me that damned line, Tim. What about you? Or will you deny that you've kept things from me? And I don't mean before I joined your team but after." He dropped back into his seat and folded his arms. "You want me to admit I screwed up? I fucking screwed up. Alien Jake got the guns, and now we have two WMDs loose." He scrubbed a hand over his face in frustration. "But this thing has taught me something." He glanced at Nessie. "A lesson someone tried to drill into me, but I was too thick-headed to grasp it right away."

Timothy took a few deep breaths. His face was still red, but his tone was more controlled when he spoke. "And what's that?"

"Everyone's got secrets, but we still have to trust one another," Daniel replied. "It's bad enough that we can't trust the Company, but if we don't trust each other, this whole thing's doomed. So, I'm coming clean, and maybe, just maybe, we should learn to trust one another if we hope to figure this shit out."

Nessie rolled her eyes, and a look of smug superiority settled on her face. "I'm glad you've finally come to see things my way."

Timothy sighed and set his stress ball down. "I'm sorry, Daniel. You're right. I screwed things up myself. I convinced myself I was creating a firewall to protect you, but maybe I've watched my ass for so long that I can't even tell friend from foe anymore." He nodded. "It takes balls to come in here and admit you screwed up, so I'll admit it, too. I should have come clean about everything I know."

Nessie cleared her throat. "As lovely as discussing your genitals is, I think we should refocus on the issue at hand— the alien. Other than brief contact with Matteas and Linda under duress, we've had little chance to communicate with them, and we have little insights into their actual goals." She frowned. "But before we discuss that, I understand how you stumbled on to the second gun, but how did you know where to look for the first?"

Daniel shrugged. "My grandfather had a connection." He looked at his mentor. "And I think you know Pops used to hunt aliens with the Army back in the day."

Timothy nodded.

Nessie scowled. "I didn't know that."

The younger agent managed a grin. "Now you do."

"I see that total trust will take a while." Nessie snorted.

"Back to the boy or alien or alien boy. He took the weapons, but what else did you glean from the encounter?"

Daniel rubbed the back of his neck. "It's not over as far as he's concerned. The guns have a control rod mechanism. My grandfather removed one from the original gun. He's yet another older man trying to protect me from myself. The alien realized it's missing. He wants it, and made it clear he'll be back for it."

Timothy's brows lowered. "And where is it now?"

"I asked my grandfather after talking to the alien. His contact, whom he said was an elf, isn't simply any elf. It's Turner Underwood."

"You're fucking kidding me." The older man groped for his stress ball again. "As in the former Fixer, the ultimate Light Elf protector of magical beings on Earth?"

"Yeah, *that* Turner Underworld." Daniel shrugged. "Or another old elf who looks like him and has that exact same name."

"Damn it. If he took the rod, there's no way he'll ever give it back. If he's involved, he's either helping Correk, the current Fixer, or he thinks there's sufficient threat that he should do this directly." He gritted his teeth. "The last thing we need is more factions involved."

"This could be a good thing," Nessie suggested.

Both men stared at her as if she'd turned into a dragon.

"We can use it to string the alien along and gain more intelligence." She frowned. "Then again, that might make him more hostile."

Daniel considered the idea. "I'm not sure. One thing I will say from talking to him is that they could be as confused about the situation as we are. He seemed taken aback that people had died because of the guns. He threatened me, but it didn't feel like a threat from the vanguard of an invasion force."

Timothy shook his head. "It could be alien Psy-Ops trying to manipulate you in different ways. If he's alien CIA, he might know how to mess with humans in ways we don't even understand."

"Maybe, but every CIA instinct I have tells me it's more complicated than that." Daniel gestured around the operations room. "If this were only about killing or exposing us, he would have done it already. Even if they don't want to use the guns, he can teleport freely. That means he could have bombed this place or even purposefully leaked the location to Fortis and bombed us both when they raided it."

"Then what do we do?" the older man asked. "Wait for an alien to show up and demand a control rod we don't have?" He tossed his stress ball a few feet down the table. "It's like Nessie said. Even if he's not hostile now, that might push him into it."

Daniel glanced at the holographic globe floating above the table. "We can't do anything but play the leads we have. Maybe if we have more artifacts and information, we'll have more leverage." He pointed to the globe. "We should hit the Australian site and see what we turn up. I understand that we must be careful because of Fortis, but we're way behind both them and the aliens now. We need a major play to catch up."

Timothy grunted, and both he and Nessie nodded.

"One last thing," he added. "Now that we're all on the same page, I need to make sure you have all the resources available." He stared at his mentor. "As we both know, my parents were most likely taken by these aliens. I don't know why. They might simply want human hostages, but my parents disappeared near a site that might have something to do with Thomas Bernard's research and alien technology. They were also looking into this extensively. My parents had journals detailing their work, including information that they were seeking a book called the *Codex of the Sky Gods.* It was something they thought would lead them to a gateway to another world. I think they found the gateway and were forced through. I have some notes and a few journals copied from at least portions of the *Codex of the Sky Gods*, including alien writing. I'll bring all the journals in. Between those and what Bernard wrote, we might make major progress."

Nessie rubbed her chin thoughtfully. "We might also be able to use that to track down the *Codex* itself or a copy. This book might have useful information that your parents weren't aware of."

Daniel shrugged. "I suppose. My parents spent years looking for it and never found the book itself."

"But they didn't have an entire team of highly trained operatives helping them, did they?" Nessie raised a brow.

Timothy snorted. "Bring the journals and the notes in, and we'll throw Ronni, Connor, and Paul at them. We need to bring on more analyst talent, now that I think of it. As for you, Daniel, I think you're right about Australia, but we should wait one more week."

Daniel frowned. "Why?"

"Because shit's getting dangerous, and you need maximum backup. John's almost up to speed, but we need to use our advantage against Fortis. They don't want to use magicals, but we have one, so we should use her."

Daniel shrugged. "Fine. Call Daisy, and we'll both go."

"She's on a personal job and will be gone for a week. Wait for her and then go." Timothy frowned. "I'd order her to come back, but she doesn't recognize my authority. There's no way in hell I'll let you go to another alien site by yourself or only with John until he's a little more knowledgeable on modern gear. We can't risk the aliens or Fortis taking you out."

He nodded. "Fine. Let's hope no aliens show up with teleporting bombs before then."

A few days later, Daniel stared at several holographic glyphs floating above the main operations room table. "What am I looking at, Ronni?"

She nibbled her lip. "Well, sir, I've looked into the translation algorithmically, along with Paul, and Connor's helped as well. Having a dedicated analyst helps a lot. We've been able to grab code and files from Project Ragnarok and Project Nephilim. Between Thomas Bernard's journals and the notes you brought in about the *Codex of the Sky Gods*, we've made progress." She tapped her portable keyboard, and a single glyph grew larger than the others. "We're sure this one means 'portal.'" She typed a few more commands. Several other glyphs grew and shrank in succession. "And we're fairly certain this series of symbols has something to do with opening a portal. But that's not the exciting part."

"What's the exciting part?"

"The location database doesn't only contain coordinates. It also has notes about the sites, all in the alien language. But in the notes corresponding to the Australia site are the symbols that relate to opening a portal. That has to mean something."

He continued to stare at the globe. "Maybe. Let's hope Daisy gets back early and we can check it out."

CHAPTER FOURTEEN

Daniel coughed as a stiff wind blew dust up from the narrow alley. Despite all the greenery and modern buildings surrounding the Nile River, his contact had insisted they meet farther east in an older part of Cairo. The entire area was choked by a maze of one- and two-story buildings in major need of a power-washing.

He preferred to be in some red-tinged dusty Australian desert looking for alien portals, but Daisy hadn't yet returned. The Company had sent him on a quick mission, one they didn't feel would even require active backup.

They had authorized a contractor, and Daniel had hired the huge shaven-headed man who now walked behind him in a gray cloak. The fashion statement was far easier to pull off in the post-Oriceran age. In this case, Jabari had made his choice based on ease of weapons concealment rather than fashion.

He grunted. "For someone who says he doesn't expect much trouble, you sure spent a lot of money and hired a dangerous man to help you."

"You know what they say, 'hope for the best and plan for the worst.'" Daniel shrugged.

In theory, the mission should unfold with little trouble. The agent needed to acquire surveillance data recorded using a magical surveillance artifact, a tiny golden falcon. While the CIA disapproved of the device, they were more than happy to take the data.

The intel would aid a deep-cover informant who was trying to infiltrate a particularly nasty, militant Humanity Defense League cell hiding in Cairo. The group was responsible for anti-Oriceran terrorist bombings, including a recent one in Algiers that had killed or injured a group of elven diplomats.

Daniel glanced over his shoulder. Jabari remained stone-faced. The man was ruthless scum and didn't value loyalty, freedom, or anything good, but he was a great asset in a fight as long as he was paid in advance.

That's the problem with these contractors. It's hard to bring them along on missions for the Codex team. Would Jabari honor his contract if he saw a transformation gun?

"How close are we?" the contractor rumbled.

Daniel tapped the side of his AR glasses. A glowing arrow and a distance readout appeared. "A few more blocks." He tapped them again to disable the overlay.

Jabari looked over his shoulder and glared at some kids kicking a soccer ball in the distance. "Just to be clear, my contract with you covers the recovery of the item. I didn't agree to escort you all the way back to the airport or anything like that."

"Yeah, yeah. I know. A contract is a contract to you,

even if it's verbal." Daniel snorted. "It must be great to not have to give a shit about anything."

"I give a shit about a lot of things but more of a shit about money." Jabari shrugged. "It's not like you work for your people for free, so you're as much a mercenary as I am."

"That's an interesting way to look at it." Daniel turned the corner. They were almost to the café where he would meet the contact and recover the falcon. He glanced around, looking for signs of surveillance. The problem was that he stood out, so more people probably watched them than not. The diversity of fashion choices among his observers also meant any of them could have concealed weapons.

The CIA needs to send me to nudist colonies only from now on.

Daniel chuckled at the thought.

"What's so funny?" Jabari asked.

"Nothing you'd care about. It doesn't have anything to do with money."

Three men stepped out of an alley about twenty yards in front of them. Their rather pale complexions and light hair set them apart even more than Daniel in a neighborhood filled with darker locals. They turned in his direction and glared at him.

He sighed. "I thought this was too easy."

Dozens of people, including children, wandered the streets, walking to and from several food stalls or the many cafes in the area. Daniel couldn't risk a fight with so much potential for collateral damage. Unlike Jabari, he did give a shit.

He grinned over his shoulder at the contractor. "Let's give these guys a little chase and make them work for their meal."

He darted into an empty alley and retrieved a sonic grenade. The contractor rushed after him, threw his cloak open, and drew a huge .50 caliber pistol. They'd made it halfway down the narrow lane when Daniel stopped. The three men hadn't followed them. They waited a few seconds but heard no heavy footfalls.

"Something's wrong," the agent muttered.

Jabari snorted. "Maybe they were tourists."

Screams erupted in the distance. They sounded like they came from the direction of the café.

Daniel shook his head and grimaced. "Shit."

He sprinted back the way they'd come and emerged from the alley. People fled in every direction, screaming and yelling. The agent increased his pace with his sonic grenade in his hand. Daniel's contact, an Egyptian man named Ali, knelt inside with his hands over his head. The three men glared at him, one aiming a gun at the man's head.

The agent raced through the fleeing crowd toward the open door and threw the sonic grenade toward the three men. It went off and the whine cut through the nearby shouts, but none of the terrorists dropped.

They spun, and all three had their pistols out. He noticed the small earbuds—anti-sonic protection.

These guys came prepared. Damn it.

Daniel jumped to the side as the men opened fire. Glass fragments from the door and window showered over him. He drew his gun and returned fire. One of the men fell with a headshot. Two loud shots behind him almost deafened him, and the two other terrorists launched backward as blood blossomed from their chests.

Jabari stepped forward and snorted. "We should have shot them to begin with."

"I was trying not to hurt innocent people in the crossfire."

"There are no innocent people, simply hunters and prey." The contractor waved toward the contact. "Hurry up. We need to go before the police or reinforcements show up."

Daniel rushed over to Ali.

The man stood, shook his head, and wiped the sweat off his brow. "I thought I was done for."

"Do you have the falcon?"

He nodded.

The agent gestured to the door. "Then let's go."

The trio ran toward the alley. The crack of rifles cut through the air, and bullets struck the street and the walls near them.

Jabari squeezed off several shots without even looking.

"Damn it, be careful," Daniel yelled. He glanced over his shoulder. Four men chased after them. Foreigners with no uniforms, he noted and assumed they were HDL members. He ducked into a side street. "Come on."

His lungs burned as he sprinted, and he wanted to laugh. His pockets were filled with gadgets from EMPs to a camera spoofer, but most were worthless for a simple run and gun fight and especially in a fight where he had to escort someone. Even if he wanted to take the falcon and leave Ali behind, according to the information he had about the artifact, he needed the man's touch to recover the data.

Sometimes, I understand why the CIA avoids magic. It can make things annoying.

Daniel grabbed a small metallic silver cylinder out of his pocket. "Ali, this is the latest model deflector." He tossed it to the other man. "Hang onto it in case I go down." He twisted a ring, and a holographic copy of himself popped up beside him. "Jabari, take him. I'll finish off the HDL bastards."

The contractor grunted and nodded. Daniel backed against the wall and raised his weapon. The terrorists appeared, and he squeezed the trigger. The first went down without firing a shot. The next three fired into his decoy, and the bullets simply passed through it and sparked against a nearby brick wall.

Daniel maintained return fire, eliminating the terrorists quickly with a satisfied grin. The ring grew warm and sparked before his decoy vanished.

He slapped it a few times, but the hologram didn't return. "Damn it. Piece of junk."

The agent frowned. It should last longer than it had, but in this case, it had served its purpose. He hurried down the street and turned to glimpse Jabari and Ali already far ahead and turning into a smaller side street.

A bullet whined past his ear, and he jumped back and flattened himself against the wall. He fired a few rounds around the corner at a new batch of adversaries. The three men all carried pistols.

He frowned. He'd expected sirens or police drones by now, but he heard nothing. Maybe the HDL had bribed the locals or disrupted the local communications somehow. He had no time to check in the middle of the fight.

I have no deflector, and my decoy's already dead. Good old-fashioned lead-slinging it is.

Daniel counted to three and hurtled around the corner. Still in motion, he ducked and fired at his enemies. He rolled behind a car parked along the street for cover and narrowly avoided a few opportunistic shots from down the street.

The car windows shattered with another volley of bullets. The vehicle jerked as a slug thudded into the side. He popped around the corner to fire and took another terrorist down, but that still left him outnumbered and too far from his contact and backup.

Shit. My contract with Jabari specified the recovery of the item, not protecting me. Once he's a few blocks away, he'll probably leave Ali and decide he did his part.

The agent's head jerked up at sudden movement from above—an incoming grenade. He leapt backward and rolled. It exploded, showering deadly fragments within a wide radius. His quick movements had saved him from death, but a few stray pieces of shrapnel sliced his leg and arm. He hopped to his feet and emptied his magazine into the two remaining terrorists. Both screamed and crumpled.

He hissed and stumbled a few feet, pain burning in his arm and leg. He retrieved an autoinjector from his now perforated jacket and shoved the device into his leg to administer a painkiller. The ache receded, and it took about half a minute before the arm pain diminished.

Daniel dragged in several deep breaths. He still had

good mobility, even with a stiff leg. The real problem was the wound to his shooting arm. He needed to catch up to Jabari and Ali. Alert for further attackers, he jogged to where he'd seen them and used the opportunity to reload.

He turned the corner, hoping to see the men, but instead, found two more armed assailants. His stiff arm slowed his response, and the men brought their pistols up first.

Damn. A half-second too slow.

Two loud gunshots deafened him and echoed in the narrow street. Both terrorists fell forward, and their weapons skidded along the asphalt. Pools of blood formed beneath them.

Daniel blinked and spotted Jabari at the corner. Smoke drifted from the barrel of his .50 caliber. Ali stood behind him, the deflector clutched in his hand and his face pale.

The CIA agent limped toward them, his leg stiffer than before. "I didn't think you'd come back for me."

Jabari snorted. "A contract is a contract. Don't you remember what the contract was?"

"Recovery of the item. But we already recovered it." Daniel nodded to Ali.

The contractor shook his head. "I was to help *you* recover the item, not this guy. If you're dead, you can't recover the item." Jabari gestured up the street. "Now, let's get out of here."

Daniel grinned. "No argument here."

They hurried down the street for another fifteen minutes. No more terrorists hounded them, and sirens sounded in the direction of the now distant café. Whether delayed by incompetence or malfeasance, the authorities had finally arrived.

Daniel exhaled sharply. "I counted at least ten guys. How many were in the cell, Ali?"

The informant shrugged. "Ten as far as I know."

"Oh, so that's that, then." Daniel leaned against a wall. "Do you still have the falcon with the intel on the terrorists?"

Jabari frowned and looked from one to the other in confusion. "If you killed all the terrorists, why do you even care?"

"That wasn't the only militant HDL cell out there."

The contractor shrugged. "You should hire me to kill them all, then. It'll save you time."

Daniel chuckled. "Maybe the CIA will take you up on that."

CHAPTER FIFTEEN

The CIA agent grimaced and rotated his arm a few times as he stepped into the dimly lit Rooney's Antiquities and Oddities. He had a few new stitches and would be stiff for a few days, but they'd told him he would suffer no permanent injury. Maybe the CIA could invest in healing potions for field agents, but he doubted that would happen anytime soon. There had to be some technological solution they could throw at the problem. Maybe he should ask Nessie.

He locked the door behind him, grateful to be home. One of the things he always appreciated about returning to America was the wide streets in most cities. He could have a proper gunfight in an American street so long as he made sure never to take down terrorists in downtown New Haven.

"No way!" Tommy shouted from the back room. "There's no damned way I can do that. You don't under-stand, Mr. Rooney."

"Calm the hell down, boy," Peter yelled in response.

Daniel rushed through the shop with a frown, utterly confused. His grandfather and Tommy had got along so well. That shouldn't have changed in a couple of days.

He ran into the back room. Tommy stood near the basement door, pacing back and forth with tears staining his cheeks. Peter was red-faced with a worried but not angry expression on his face.

"What the hell is going on?" Daniel asked.

The other two snapped their heads in his direction.

Tommy wiped his tears. "I can't do it. Don't make me do it. I've heard how they treat half-Oricerans."

The agent frowned. "What are you talking about?"

The half-elf dropped into a chair and lowered his head to the table.

Peter sighed and ran a hand through his hair. "One of his neighbors noticed his dad wasn't home. They called Child Protective Services, and a social worker stopped by his place. Now they're talking about sending him into foster care or a group home."

The teen slapped his palm on the table without lifting his head. "I can't go into the system. It's not fair. Dad will be back tomorrow. I told them that, and they didn't care. *He* called them and told them, but they still didn't care." He lifted his head and wiped away more tears. "What can I do?"

Daniel frowned. "You said your dad will be home tomorrow?"

Tommy nodded despairingly.

"Then you'll do nothing. I'll talk to your father tomorrow. He needs to take point on this, and I'll make sure he does."

Daniel didn't bother to hide the menace in his voice, but Tommy barely noticed.

This farce had continued long enough.

———

The next afternoon, Daniel banged on the door of Tommy's apartment. He'd asked the boy to stay at the shop while he talked to his father. Even if the half-elf didn't know it, Daniel wasn't sure this wouldn't end in a few well-placed blows.

No one answered. Daniel followed up with a few more loud raps.

"I'm coming, dude," called a mellow voice from inside. "Keep your fucking pants on."

Daniel gritted his teeth.

Time to practice a little self-control. If I beat his ass, it won't help Tommy, and I'll land in jail. Tim and Nessie would love that.

The door swung open to reveal a lean, shirtless elf in tight leather pants that left little to the imagination. The family resemblance to Tommy was striking, even down to the one gray and one blue eye. The man's long, dark hair hung to his small of his back. His full-blood was far more obvious in his pointed ears.

"Erik, right?" Daniel asked. "I've seen you around the neighborhood, but we've never really talked."

Tommy's father stared at Daniel for a moment with a confused look on his face before recognition dawned and he smiled. "Oh, yeah, I know you. Daniel Winters. That dude everyone calls 'the mayor.' You're champion of the neighborhood and shit. I heard you beat up muggers and some dude fucking with Charlie's dog."

Daniel nodded slowly. "Can I come in?"

Erik motioned inside. "Sure, dude."

Daniel narrowed his eyes as he stepped into the living room. Clothes were strewn all over the floor and furniture, obviously Erik's, judging by the size. A drum set occupied the corner. Posters of various metal bands, modern and classic, decorated the room, including Trevilsom, Sons of Gwar, Black Sabbath Reborn, Six Feet Under, and Seven Deadly Sins.

A half-eaten McDonald's hamburger lay in its wrapper on a coffee table covered with clothes.

How did this guy make such a mess? He just got back.

Daniel closed the door behind him, thinking about how quickly certain people could go native. Erik was either very young for an elf or had thrown himself wholeheartedly into a certain perceived identity. It wouldn't be the first time, though it did make him question how much of Daisy's persona was performance versus reality.

He folded his arms. "Your son is inches away from being sent into foster care or a group home."

Erik dropped onto his torn leather couch. "Yeah, yeah. That's the *man* trying to scare him." He waved a hand dismissively. "He's fine. He's not starving or anything."

Daniel frowned. "Abandoning your kid for long periods is enough to get CPS involved."

"Nah, nah. He's fine." The elf shook his head and shrugged, the confused expression returning to his face. Some people had a resting bitch face. He had a resting idiot face. "And he was, like, staying with you half the time, right, dude? What am I supposed to do? Not work?"

"It isn't about not working. It's about making sure your son is taken care of." Daniel took a deep breath and let it out slowly. Erik might not have a punchable face, but he had a punchable mouth.

"I asked that bitch from CPS if I could take him on tour with me, and she asked me all this shit about tutors and stuff. What the fuck? I can't afford a tutor." Erik shrugged. "School's not important anyway. Tommy's gonna be a musician. You don't need bullshit school for that."

Daniel shook his head. "He doesn't want to be a musician. He wants to go into robotics. He definitely needs bullshit school for that."

Erik snorted. "Robotics? That's soulless." He slapped his chest. "The blood of a Light Elf runs through him. Music is part of our very being. Not only that, he's half-human, so he gets to grow up around music that we would never have even thought of on Oriceran. Heavy metal? There ain't no metal on Oriceran." His eyes widened, and he stared at the ceiling with a look of ecstasy on his face. "I don't get it. The music is everything, dude. I've tried to be a good dad and not pressure him or force him into something, even though I think he'd make a wicked bass player, but he keeps whining."

Daniel shrugged. "Because he doesn't want to be a fucking musician. This isn't exactly rocket science."

Erik blinked several times. "Maybe you could talk to him, dude. You're the mayor, and he likes your comics and shit. He'll listen to you. Tell him to stop being a whining pussy."

The agent curled his fists and took a few steps toward the elf but managed to restrain himself. If the man had laid a hand on the boy, it'd be an easy decision. Daniel would have taught him a thing or two about respecting his son. Hitting Erik now would only involve the cops and upset Tommy, who loved his father even if the man was a negligent piece of shit.

"You don't even care, do you?" Daniel muttered through gritted teeth. "If CPS throws him into foster care or a group home, you don't care because it's only about the music for you."

Erik shook his head. "A man has to follow his passion. Tommy will be okay. Sometimes, life is there to inspire the music. Suffering can make great art, dude."

Daniel snorted and spun on his heel. He threw the door open.

"Where you going?" the elf called. "I thought we were talking."

He stopped in the doorway and chuckled darkly. "I'm leaving before I do something we both regret." He stepped out and slammed the door, rattling the nearby windows with the force of it.

Tommy didn't have a chance with a father like that. Daniel stomped down the stairs leading to the street, shaking his head. There was one possibility, but he wasn't sure if it was a good idea.

But at least, he reasoned, it was better than this.

When he returned to the shop an hour later, his grandfather was out on a Fresca run. Tommy sat in the back room thumbing through an older issue of Batman. The cover depicted the Caped Crusader standing on the edge of a building in Tokyo framed by Tokyo Tower in the background. Daniel still remembered the exact date he'd bought the comic: July 5th, 2024. Old paper and ink still brought joy to a new generation.

The boy looked up from the comic. "I'm sorry I cried earlier. I didn't mean to be a baby, dude. I'll be tougher next time."

Daniel shook his head. "You're not the one who is at fault. Your father should step up, but I couldn't get through to him. He's too damned obsessed with his music."

The boy sighed and slumped in his chair. "So that's it? I'm going into the system."

Daniel shook his head. "No. Absolutely not."

Tommy looked up and shrugged. "It's not like I want to. Around here, people know me and like me, but I've been in places where people look at me, call me an Ori, and tell me to go back to my own planet even though I was born here. It doesn't matter. I know several kids—all full humans—in foster care or in group homes. If you're different, if you stand out, they mess with you." He shrugged. "I can't change what I am, dude. I'm screwed."

"You're not thinking of other possibilities." Daniel leaned against the wall and folded his arms.

"What other possibilities? Running away? I'm not gonna eat from garbage cans and sleep in parks." Tommy's shoulders slumped. "Maybe I'll get lucky. You know, find a nice family or something and not have to go to a group home."

Daniel chuckled.

Tommy's head snapped up. "This isn't funny!"

"I know it isn't." The agent smiled gently. "You've missed the obvious." He pointed to the folded-up cot in the corner of the room. "CPS wants you somewhere stable where a responsible adult can look after you."

The boy's eyes widened. "No way."

Daniel nodded. "Yeah. Now, I'll be honest with you. If it were only me, they probably wouldn't agree because I leave the country too often, but Pops is retired—or semi-retired, anyway—and here all the time. This is a solid business with at least one stable adult here every day. I talked with the social worker before coming home and explained my offer. She said it's fine. Pops, as the primary responsible adult, will have to fill out most of the paperwork, but I already called him and he agreed. He'll be back soon. It took him longer than he thought because he had to go to three stores to find his Fresca."

Tommy blinked a few times and wiped away tears of joy. "T-thanks, dude. I just…thanks."

"You're welcome." Daniel pushed off the wall. "But there will be some changes."

"Oh, yeah, sure. If you need me to mop or do your laundry or whatever, I'll do it." Tommy shrugged.

"Slow down there, Cinderella." The agent shook his head. "That's not what I meant. Stability means actual *stability*, not sleeping in a cot in a back room like a reject from *Harry Potter*. You'll sleep on the couch for now. When I'm out of town, you can use my bed like before, but we'll replace the couch upstairs with a sleeper sofa. It'll be cramped, but I think it's a better deal than ending up in the system or sleeping on a cot."

Tommy grinned and nodded before his grin disappeared. "I thought of one thing that will suck about the new set-up."

"And what's that?"

The boy nodded to a rack of comics with a serious expression on his face. "Not waking up with the heroes."

***

Daniel stifled a yawn as he made his way out of his room. He glanced at Tommy, who snored quietly on the couch. He had never intended for the boy to end up a permanent resident when he'd first offered to let him stay in the back room, but it really did seem to be the best solution.

Peter peeked around the corner and gestured for Daniel to join him. He ducked back down the hallway and into his room.

Daniel arched a brow and followed his grandfather. "What's up?"

The old man sighed. "I want you to understand that I really like the boy, I do. And I want him to be okay."

"But?"

"I also want us to think about whether this is the best thing for him."

Daniel shrugged. "Sending him into the system wouldn't be the best thing, and his father's useless. Someone has to look out for him, and I don't see why it shouldn't be us." He frowned. "I don't get it. You already agreed to sign the paperwork. Why are you objecting now?"

"We're involved in dangerous stuff," Peter replied. "Very dangerous stuff. I'm an old man. It doesn't matter if I die, but what about the boy?"

The agent sighed. "I've thought about it a lot. If Tommy had another choice I'd push him that way, but for now, we're his best option." He pointed to a picture of his mother on the desk in the corner. "I was lucky when I was a teen. My parents didn't choose to leave me, but it felt the same. If you weren't around, I would have ended up as a ward of the state. I would have been tossed around from family to family, but you were there to remind me that someone gave a damn about me, and that's one of the reasons I'm the man I am today."

Peter sucked in a breath and nodded slowly. "You're right, but you have to promise me that if you ever think Tommy's in danger, you'll do everything you can to protect him, even if it pisses Tim or the CIA off."

"Of course I will, Pops, even if that means I have to hide him in the brownstone under a pile of chameleon balls."

Peter turned away and rubbed at a hint of a tear in his eye.

"Is there a problem, Pops?"

Peter snorted. "I don't dust enough in here. I got a little something in my eye, is all."

Daniel smiled and turned away. "Then I'll leave you to your dusting."

CHAPTER SIXTEEN

"The dozens of zombies lumber toward you," Connor announced as he peered over his dungeon master's screen. He moved some figurines on the table. "Consider each of these to represent four zombies. The clunk of the grate echoes through the small chamber. There's no escape." He grinned at Daniel. "Do you regret using up so many spells earlier on the Wights?"

"The warrior was paralyzed. I didn't have a choice." Daniel shrugged. "And we'll be fine. We're taking on a bunch of undead with a high-level priest." He nodded toward Taylor.

"I'm so confident that I don't even move forward to engage the zombies," Juan stated.

Lorelai nodded quickly, her red curls bouncing from the motion. "I'll stay in the corner away from them."

The other three players looked at Taylor with expectant faces.

He grinned. "Yeah. This is why I wanted to take on the

necropolis quest. I stride forward, hold up my holy symbol, and turn the undead."

Connor scoffed. "You haven't won yet." His eyes gleamed with mischief. "Hey, who wants to make this a real challenge?"

"What do you mean?"

Connor gulped some Fresca, this time in a non-cake and non-alcoholic form. It was one of the few times Daniel hadn't seen him drinking alcohol at a recent session.

The dungeon master picked up a blue crystal twenty-sided die. "How about I make the saving throw for the whole group instead of individually?"

Juan laughed and slapped his knee. "Do it, man. Take the gamble."

Daniel eyed Connor. "That benefits you more than him."

The DM shook his head. "Nope. Not really. The odds are on his side. We're talking zombies versus a level-eight cleric."

Everyone looked at Taylor and waited breathlessly.

He shrugged. "Why the hell not?"

Connor snatched the single die, cupped it in both hands, and shook it. Two seconds passed. Four. Ten.

"Get on with it!" everyone shouted at once.

He threw and grimaced.

Taylor chuckled and looked from the die to Connor. He pointed to the figurines. "It looks like they're all within range to me. Feel the holy wrath, you zombie mother-fuckers."

Connor muttered under his breath and grabbed the figurines. "You utter your prayer, the divine light of your deity fills the room, and the searing glow reduces the zombies to ash."

Juan high-fived Taylor. "Damn. Too bad that shit doesn't work in real life."

"Are we sure it doesn't?" Lorelai asked. "Like, has any priest tried that with zombies? I know they had that big necromancer down in Mexico who caused trouble. I wonder what happened to him. Maybe a few priests turned some undead."

Connor shook his head and packed the zombie figurines away. "Why don't we take a little break?"

Lorelai smirked. "What, are you pouting because your gamble didn't pay off? Don't be such a whiner, Connor."

He grunted and shrugged.

She leaned forward, her smile growing wider. "If you're interested in getting your gamble on, then I have just the thing. I have my own For Want of a Dollar challenge."

Connor's eyes gleamed, and he rubbed his hands together. "Okay, I'm on a roll."

"You just failed a roll."

"Nope. I'm on a roll when it comes to For Want of a Dollar."

Daniel laughed. "I don't think one counts as 'a roll.'"

"Then it's time to make it two for two."

Taylor and Juan nodded, their faces eager.

Lorelai fished out her phone. "I'll show you a series of pictures of things from Oriceran, and you have to tell me whether or not they are actual foods. I'll go one dollar for one dollar for each question."

Daniel smiled. They always talked a big game about their challenges but considering what inflation had done to the dollar in the last twenty years, it was amazing anyone could buy anything useful. Worldwide economic instability had also spiked immediately after the truth about Oriceran came out, which didn't help. But betting without skin in the game was pointless, and they needed some way to keep score.

"I hate to be that guy," he offered, "but there are intelligent species on Oriceran who aren't even humanoid, and even the ones who are can eat things that humans can't."

Lorelai smiled. "When I say foods, I mean something a human could eat and digest without magical assistance. I saw these on an episode of *Diners, Dives, and Dragons with Guy Fieri Junior* and he ate all of them."

Daniel nodded. "Fair enough. I'm ready, then."

Lorelai fixed each man in turn with a serious look. She swiped her phone and held it up. The picture showed a bowl containing a thick, red, glowing, lumpy liquid with several tentacles visible.

"Shall we do secret votes?" Taylor asked.

She shook her head. "Sometimes, it's fun to see who is brave and who isn't."

Juan narrowed his eyes and leaned forward. "I'm voting yes. I think it's their version of calamari and probably invigorated with magic."

Taylor rubbed his chin. "Me, too."

Lorelai looked at Daniel. "What about you?"

He stared at the picture for several seconds and shook his head.

"No," Daniel replied. "Do I have to guess what it is?"

"Nope," Lorelai replied. She glanced at Connor. "You're the last one."

Connor shook his head. "No."

Juan snorted. "He's copying Daniel."

"We'll make him go first on the next one." Lorelai grinned. "Everyone ready for the answer?"

The men all nodded.

"It's not food." Lorelai declared. "It's a pet. It lives in that liquid and looks like a Furby crossed with a squid."

"Damn. Bring on the next one," Juan blurted.

She swiped again and held up a new picture. Daniel frowned. From what he could tell, it resembled a roasted chicken breast, but the angle might conceal something.

"Go." Lorelai snapped her gaze to Connor.

"Obviously food. Too easy."

"Yeah," Juan offered.

Taylor nodded his agreement.

Daniel shrugged. "Food."

"Yep." Lorelai smiled. "I thought I'd try to trick you, but if you saw the actual bird, you'd be surprised anyone would think to eat it. It's seriously ugly and has three eyes."

"People eat poison fish on our planet, and shit, even octopuses and squid," Juan replied.

Everyone chuckled.

A few more questions passed, both yes and no, with Lorelai winning most of her bets though Connor continued his streak.

He stood and, despite not having had any alcohol, did a silly dance. His sobriety relative to the others could explain his winning streak, Daniel decided. He held second place with a few misses, but Juan and Taylor were destroyed.

Lorelai made a grand gesture with her arms. "Gentleman, time for the final question." She swiped her phone again and held up a picture of a translucent blue crystal covered in sharp-edged points.

Juan shook his head, grimacing. "I think their dentists use that. Not food."

"Yeah, I agree with him," Taylor commented.

Daniel rubbed his chin and stared at the picture. Lorelai said the items were all things humans could digest, but the crystal looked downright dangerous.

"No."

Lorelai nodded gravely and turned toward Connor. "Will you continue to be a champion or will you join the ranks of the losers?"

Juan snorted. "Losers?"

Connor threw up a hand. "Silence, loser." He grinned. "And I'm ready to continue being a champion. I declare that...actual food!"

Everyone stared at the grinning Lorelai, waiting for her revelation.

"And it is..." She stood, a triumphant look on her face. "*Food!*"

Connor's fist pumped and slapped his chest. "I am a champion! Booyah."

Juan shook his head. "No way anyone can eat that."

Lorelai took four white paper wrappers from her purse. She tossed one to each man. Everyone snatched theirs in the air with ease, except for Connor, the only sober one of the group. He muttered and grabbed it off the floor.

The papers rustled as they were unwrapped to reveal the blue crystals from the final bet.

"This will shred my mouth," Juan complained.

Lorelai rolled her eyes. "Grow a pair and try it."

Daniel plucked his crystal from the wrapper and let the paper float to the ground. "Do I chew or what?"

"Just pop it in and suck."

Connor smirked. "That's what she s—"

He shut his mouth at Lorelai's glare.

Daniel shrugged and tossed the Oriceran crystal in his mouth. The sharp edges melted away immediately and released an earthy, herbal taste that coated his tongue. The candy, as he thought of it, continued to disintegrate in his mouth. A few seconds later, a rich umami flavor spilled out, followed by an acidic counterpoint, then finally, a tangy but sweet taste.

He blinked a few times and swallowed the small amount of liquid left. At this point, only hints of the final flavor remained.

"That's different. It kind of has everything, but it's not bad." Daniel shrugged.

Lorelai nodded. "Yeah. The species which make them actually has a cooler body temperature than humans, so it takes a lot longer for the whole flavor cycle. My understanding that is their sense of taste is different, too, so it's almost like a spiritual experience for them."

The other men swallowed their candies, their expressions shifting from skeptical to happily surprised.

Connor swallowed. "Have you got another one? I want to mix it with Fresca."

Daniel strolled into Timothy's office at the brownstone, his shoulders relaxed. Though Jake's threat still hung over him, he'd not seen the boy and nor had any of the Codex team. Whatever plan the alien had, he took his time and let Daniel live his life in the interim. The agent wouldn't let himself forget that Jake was out there, but he also wouldn't worry.

Timothy looked seriously pensive behind his desk.

And there goes my relaxation.

Daniel dropped into a chair. "Your text said you needed to see me, but that it wasn't urgent."

The older man nodded. "Yes. There's more talk at the Company about using you as bait for Morgana and soon, but I've also seen movement from people who might be associated with Fortis."

"Meaning?"

Timothy shrugged. "It could mean nothing, or it could mean they'll set you up as bait for Morgana and kill you after you've served their purpose. I don't have proof, but my gut tells me to be careful. I've lived this long because I trust my gut."

Daniel thought that over for a few seconds before responding. "If Fortis wanted me dead, why not have Troy shoot me and then blame the Russians?"

"I'm not sure. Maybe it wasn't the right time."

The agent sighed. "What do you recommend?"

"Take control of this so Fortis can't set you up. Push your contacts to resolve the Morgana issue. You can still use official CIA resources, but if you head the investigation yourself, you can set the tempo." Timothy frowned and thought for a moment. "Plus, if you're doing this, it'll reduce the likelihood that they'll task you with other missions. You'll then potentially have a better chance to respond if Jake makes a move."

Daniel laughed. "So, in other words, I should throw myself into tracking down some twisted magical serial killer who harvests people's organs and who wants a piece of me so I can make time in case the alien who is mad at me wants to come at me."

Timothy grunted. "Yes. That about sums it up."

"Beats being bored." Daniel shrugged.

CHAPTER SEVENTEEN

It took ten minutes of waiting for the special stall with the secret entrance to Lucky's to become available. It wasn't the first time he'd had to wait, the inevitable pitfall of the elaborate entrance system. Daniel pushed his irritation aside as he made his way down the darkened stairwell.

He took a deep breath as he stepped into the main room and looked around. Hoodlums, thugs, and ne'er-do-wells ranging from short gnomes to huge Kilomea filled every round table, and as always, the low illumination left plenty of deep shadows for the questionable to hide in. Sometimes, Daniel wondered what the place would look like with decent lighting.

The agent stopped for a moment, immediately tense. An elf with an X-shaped scar sat at a table playing cards with a frowning gnome. He narrowed his eyes.

Saram? But he's dead.

A few seconds later, the tension seeped from his body. It wasn't Saram. Even though the gambling elf had a similar scar, every other feature from the shape of his nose to his eye color was different. Saram wouldn't fake his own death and return in a disguise that included a prominent feature of his previous appearance.

Daniel headed over to the bar. He needed to obey Rule #2 and buy at least one drink. He took a seat on a stool and waited as Lucky moved from the other end of the bar, a huge smile on his face.

The proprietor adjusted his tie and the lapels of his pinstripe suit. He grabbed a glass already filled with a drink from beneath the bar—a whiskey sour. With a grin, he set the drink down in front of Daniel.

The bartender smiled. "Hey, Daniel, my *paisano*. Have this drink."

"For free?" Daniel raised an eyebrow.

Lucky released a barking laugh.

"I thought so." Daniel took a small sip. "Any trouble lately?"

Lucky snorted. "Nah. People ain't going to be that dumb in my place. It's been a while since I've had to teach anyone a lesson." He nodded toward an elf in a dark suit with twin daggers hanging from matching sheaths. He was one of the many men Lucky used to enforce order in his place. Other deadly men lingered in various corners.

"Good to hear." Daniel stood, his drink in hand, and nodded to Lucky. "Put it on my tab."

"Sure. You be careful. Glad to see those HDL bastards didn't whack you in Cairo." Lucky gestured a cut across his neck with his finger.

Of course, he knows about that.

Daniel chuckled and shook his head. He maneuvered between the tables, avoiding a busty human waitress in black heels and a miniscule skirt. After another small sip, he surveyed the bar slowly, looking for someone who might be useful.

His gaze settled on a familiar smile capped with two gold teeth. Ralph. The owner of the smile also wore a purple velvet suit. Daniel hid his instinctive frown. As much as the man made his skin crawl at times, he'd provided useful info in their last few encounters.

The agent made his way to Ralph's table. "Mind if I join you?"

The man gestured to an empty chair and sipped his Manhattan. "*Mi casa, su casa* and all that."

"I'm interested in information." He set his drink down and took a seat. "And that's allegedly still your business."

The informant grinned at him. "Damn right it is, and I'm moving up in the world." He tugged at the lapels of his jacket. "As you can see."

More money doesn't mean better taste, asshole.

Daniel leaned forward and forced his hand out of his pocket. Rule #4 prohibited his instinct to use a silence cube, though Rule #5 made it less important.

"Morgana," he declared.

Ralph nodded, his grin widening. "The Queen of Hearts? Not simply off with their heads, but out with their hearts, lungs, brains, and everything else, huh? That's some messed-up shit, even in a world filled with messed-up shit."

The CIA man pushed his drink to the side. "I'm glad you agree, and I want to do something about it, but I need to find her first. She likes to keep a low profile, but I bet a man like you who is moving up in the world has heard things—things you'd be willing to share for a not so insignificant amount of money. No barter today, merely straight coin if you're interested."

"Money's the real magic in this world, and I always need more." Ralph sipped his drink, avarice gleaming in his eyes. "Show me some good faith first." He pulled his phone from his pocket, tapped in a few commands, and flipped it so Daniel could see the crypto wallet address on the screen.

He nodded, his phone ready, and initiated a transfer of Trollcoin. "That's foot-in-the-door money. I want to hear what you've got."

The other man smiled. "Well, I don't know where she is, exactly."

Daniel narrowed his eyes. "Are you fuckin' with me, Ralph?"

"What if I am?" He leaned forward. "Whatcha gonna do about it? Are you gonna go after me in Lucky's and violate Rule #1? Huh? I'd like to see that shit." He chuckled. "I dare you to do it. You can kill me, but you're dead before you leave."

Don't tempt me.

The agent smiled without humor. "I'd think you would want to keep a potential return customer happy. You know I have good money backing me, and that money can be yours for as long as you are useful."

"Yeah, yeah," Ralph smirked. "Look, Daniel. Don't wet your panties. It's true I don't know where she is, but I know somebody who does. I heard about her recently." He tapped the side of his head. "And I filed that shit away in here because I knew it'd be useful. And here we are."

"I don't get it," Daniel scoffed and shook his head. "Not all that long ago, you were small-time, and now, you have information that I'd practically have to kill someone to get normally."

"I guess you underestimated me, but because of that little crack about me being small-time, you now have to pay ten percent more. Base price ten times what you already sent me." Ralph chuckled. "Anyway, I'm only a man who knows how to be in the right place at the right time."

"In other words, you're lucky?"

Ralph laughed. "Yeah, that's the shit. I'm lucky."

Daniel stared at the man, burning curiosity poking through with numerous questions as to what had fueled Ralph's transformation, but that was a mystery for another day. He needed to focus. He initiated another money transfer.

You better not fuck with me. If you do, you better run and hide right after this.

Ralph's phone beeped with the transfer notification, and he sucked air in through his teeth. "Better than fuck-ing." He tapped at his phone for a minute before placing it on the table. Grinning with a smugness that was almost ugly, he leaned forward and reached into his jacket.

Daniel watched him carefully but remained motionless. Ralph surprised him with a pen and paper.

The informant scribbled down a name and phone number and slid it over to the agent. Julia Eddington, Daniel noted. "You might want to go to Jolly Old England before you make the call. That's where she lives right now. I would hurry, though. Your girl won't be there long. She knows the Queen of Hearts, and from what I hear, she's looking for people who don't like her." He winked. "Good luck on not getting harvested."

A loud gunshot rang out, and Daniel dropped to the ground, his hand going instinctively for his gun.

Ralph jerked back and knocked his Manhattan over. The drink spilled all over the table. "Motherfucker."

Every conversation in the room died as people looked around for the source of the shot.

Lucky stood in front of the bar with a shotgun in hand, the barrel pointed at a body in a pool of blood.

"Listen the fuck up," he shouted, gesturing with the gun toward the huge hole in the man's chest. "And look at his fucking hands."

Daniel stood to see better. The dead man clutched a gun. A surprised-looking man at a table right in front of him stared at the weapon.

Lucky tossed the shotgun on the bar. "I have a lot of rules. I know I do, but the first is simple. If you have a grudge about a fucking mission, you stow it at the fucking door. No battles and no deaths unless it's my men or me doing the killing." He gestured dismissively at the dead man. "This piece of trash thought he could do a hit in my place. He thought he could ignore my rules." He shook his head. "*No one* ignores my rules. Not only did he try to break Rule #1, but he had the balls to tell someone a few minutes ago that Bocelli was a better tenor than Pavarotti. So, he broke two rules, and he'd not bought a drink yet, so that's three. Dumbass piece-of-shit fucktard." After adjusting his jacket, he snorted and waved at the corpse. "Clean that garbage up." He hopped back over the bar and slid his shotgun beneath the counter. His casual smile returned as if he'd not gunned a man down moments before.

Two of his guards rushed over and picked up the body, then moved toward a barely visible black door hidden in the shadows and disappeared. A waitress stepped out of the same door with a cleaning bot and set the square robot near the bloodstain. She pressed a few buttons and walked away as the machine sprayed cleaning fluid and began its work.

Everyone else returned their attention to their drinks or their tablemates.

Ralph snorted. "Some people are born dumbasses."

"I can't argue with that." Daniel stared as the cleaning bot hummed along, spraying and mopping up the blood.

I doubt whoever invented those expected them to be used for that.

Daniel yawned as he stepped into the W&M less than twelve hours after his trip to Lucky's. He smirked and couldn't help but compare the two places. The upscale London bar hosted distinguished-looking professionals in suits. There wasn't a single X-shaped scar among them.

He glanced over his shoulder as Daisy entered with an easy smile on her face. She'd finished her job, which turned out to be in France, so it was easy for her to arrive and back him up. The elf woman was dressed conservatively for once, which meant a tight leather jacket and leather pants rather than a catsuit. Her outfit provided a high sartorial contrast to Daniel's dapper suit.

"I love this place," Daisy murmured. "You can hear yourself think."

The agent chuckled. "Too well-lit for a lot of business, though. It keeps the cockroaches away, and sometimes, we need to follow them." He surveyed the bar and his gaze settled on a skinny, short-haired woman in a corner booth —Julia Eddington, according to the picture she'd sent. "I see her."

"Then let's find out where your jilted ex-girlfriend is," Daisy smirked.

Daniel moved toward Julia. "I think I'd remember if I dated a woman who liked to harvest organs."

"Sometimes, women have hobbies they don't share with their boyfriend."

The woman looked at them with a frown and nodded to the seats opposite her.

"Do you mind if I make our conversation private?" Daniel asked.

Julia shrugged. "Go ahead."

He activated his silence cube and placed it on the table. The light rock and chatter permeating the bar vanished.

"I've been told you can help me find Morgana," he said with a smile.

Julia's face twitched. "I can, but before I tell you, I want to know why you're looking for her."

Daniel scoffed. "She's a psychopath who needs to be stopped, isn't that a good enough reason? I already gave you half-payment for the information. You play cute now, and you won't see anything else from me."

Daisy clucked her tongue and leaned back.

Julia sighed and looked away. "Look, she's dangerous. I should know, we used to…work together."

The agent narrowed his eyes. "You worked with Morgana?"

She grabbed her multi-colored, floral-pattern macramé handbag, set it on the table, and held it open. "Look."

Daniel tilted his head to peer inside at a wand.

"You're a witch."

Daisy's eyebrows rose, and a small smile played on her lips.

Julia nodded. "I specialize in life magic."

"Just like the Kardashians," replied Daniel.

She rolled her eyes. "They aren't the only life witches in history, you know. Anyway, Morgana and I used to do magical research together, but she didn't like the results she had with her existing magic, so she decided to walk another path."

"Let me guess: necromancy," Daisy muttered.

Julia nodded. "Yes. Necromancy. She's twisted and evil now, completely fucked up. Not only that, she's powerful. She can body hop, among other things."

Daniel snorted. "If you hate what she's become so much, why haven't you stopped her?"

"Because I can't!" Julia yelled. She closed her eyes and sighed before opening them again. "She's too powerful for me, and she knows my magic too well. The one time I tried to go after her, I barely escaped with my life. You must understand, with Morgana, killing you is probably the nicest thing she can do to you. But I still keep my ear to the ground. I heard you were looking for her, and I might be able to help you out with her location." She held up a hand. "I don't know it right now, but I know where to look. This isn't a shakedown. I don't even want more money. I merely wanted to make sure you were serious about this."

Daniel nodded. "We're damned serious."

"Okay, then, but you have to promise me one thing."

"What?"

Julia licked her lips. "I don't want to be anywhere near her when you go after her."

"Fair enough," he replied.

Daisy cleared her throat. "Did she ever mention a man named Daniel to you?"

Julia frowned and glanced at the agent. "Like him?"

He shrugged. "I've heard she's left some threats with my name on them." He hadn't given Julia's his real last name. The CIA agent had no reason to trust her so implicitly.

The witch shook her head. "I knew her for years, and I don't ever remember her mentioning someone named Daniel. I have no idea why she cares about you. Look, can we wrap this up?"

"Fine. You have my contact number. If you can tell me where she is, contact me. Even if you don't want the money, I'll be happy to pay you."

She breathed deeply a few times, grabbed her wand, and muttered an incantation under her breath.

Daisy frowned and narrowed her eyes. "What spell are you casting?"

Julia turned her free palm up as a blood sigil formed in her hand. "A binding spell." She half-closed her eyes. "I invoke the blood magic to bind me to this man Daniel." The mark glowed bright red. "It'll allow you to track me with magic and always find me…or my body if she kills me before I can contact you." She held her hand out.

Daniel shook it, and warmth seeped into his palm for a second.

Daisy frowned at him.

When the witch withdrew her hand, the bloody imprint had faded. "Are you sure about finding Morgana? I would be happy to see her finally die, but I'm not sure it's possible."

He snorted. "There's nothing on this world or Oriceran that can't be defeated. She has challenged me more than once, so I have no choice but to respond and finish this."

Julia shoved her wand back in her handbag and stood. "If you'll excuse me, I'd like to get back to my apartment." Her eyes darted around nervously. "I need to be where there are protective wards in place. I shouldn't have done this here, but I didn't realize she had targeted you. That means she could be hunting you and might actually be near." She shuddered.

Daniel grabbed her arm. "I'll end this, Julia. Don't worry."

She jerked her arm away. "I'll do my best to get you the information, but I'll be honest. It'll likely be weeks before I find anything."

"I'm willing to wait. Contact me when you have a lead, and I'll take it from there."

Julia snorted. "I will if I'm still alive." She hurried toward the door.

A line of glyphs glowed on Daisy's arm, and she whispered something under her breath. "Let's see…"

Daniel flashed her an inquiring look. "See what?"

"If she was telling the truth…hmmm. Yes, she's established a link between you and her. I'm not sure that was wise." The elf sighed.

"A link? It goes both ways, right?"

She nodded. "Yes. That's why I think it's a bad idea."

Daniel shrugged. "Will it break if she kills me?"

Daisy shook her head. "Not immediately, but it'll fade quicker."

"There's a simple solution, then. Kill her if she kills me."

She laughed. "Confident, aren't we?"

"We need a lead on Morgana." Daniel studied his hand, half-expecting a blood sigil to form. "And if a little risk is what it takes, I'll do it. This was the Company's plan anyway—dangle a Daniel and see if a killer bites."

"The spell means I'll have to suppress the magic if you don't want her to track you to somewhere you don't want her to know about." More symbols appeared on Daisy's arms, and she motioned rapidly with her hands. "There. I've sealed it for now, but I'll have to refresh it at some point. Her spell won't last forever, and I won't break it until she's served her purpose."

Daniel looked at the door, but the witch had long since departed. "I assume it'll be weeks before we get any useful intel on Morgana. So much for handling this quickly."

The elf grinned, and her eyebrows lifted teasingly. "Well, I know something fun we could do in the meantime."

He maintained a serious expression, although his imagination stirred. "And what would that be?"

"We could go to Australia."

Daniel stared at her for a second before he nodded quickly. "Of course, of course."

Daisy eyed him with a mischievous smile. "What did you *think* I meant?"

He gestured vaguely. "Something like that. You're right. We need to get a flight and ship our equipment there ahead of us."

She stepped out of the booth and licked her lips. "There's one other thing we could do first."

Okay, now she's messing with me.

"What?" Daniel asked.

Daisy winked. "Get some lunch."

Definitely *messing with me.*

Jake watched Daisy and Daniel as they walked out of the W&M, confident his cloaking field would shield him against detection. The CIA agent on the move meant an increased chance of discovering the location of the missing control rod.

Without the gun, the control rod was useless, so that at least gave him time. Even if they didn't need the rod, it was a good excuse to watch Daniel. The agent pretended to be dedicated to justice at the brownstone, but Jake knew he would slip up eventually and reveal himself as a monster like so many of his CIA friends.

Humans couldn't be trusted. They were a barbarous species, violent and rapacious. He would never let himself forget that.

CHAPTER EIGHTEEN

The sparse clouds allowed Daniel to peer out the side window at the sprawling, red-tinged, shrub-covered Outback that spread for hundreds of miles below. It was beautiful and harsh at the same time. An occasional mesa or mountain poked up from the ground, adding texture to the landscape.

It wasn't the first time he'd been to Australia, but it was the first time he'd flown over it in a small four-seater jet.

He shook his head at Daisy in the pilot's seat. She wore her headset and AR pilot goggles, along with a bright smile. Her hands rested on the plane's yoke.

"We have about an hour until we reach the coordinates," she announced. The roar of the engine swallowed her voice, but the headset mic transmitted it to his ears without trouble. "I'm glad Tim arranged a VTOL plane. It makes this easy, although a helicopter would have worked too, even if it is slower."

Daniel shook his head. "I still can't believe it."

"Oh, are you still sulking because you didn't know I could fly a plane?" Daisy smirked.

"It's not that you can fly a plane. You can do magic, and that's more impressive than flying a plane or a helicopter. It's simply that I never *knew* you could fly, even after we've worked together for ages."

"A girl has to have some secrets."

"Do you have any other secret skills I should know about?"

The plane shuddered slightly and Daisy steadied the yoke, leveling it gently. "I can juggle."

Daniel laughed. "Juggle, seriously?"

"Yes, and I don't use magic. I mean regular old juggling."

"Why that?" he wondered.

She shrugged. "Why not? You never know when a skill will come in handy."

The CIA agent stared at her for a moment as his thoughts jostled with the new information. "There's a lot more to you than I ever realized."

Her smile faded for a moment. "Of course there is. I'm a lot older than you." She glanced his way as if assessing his reaction. "And I've had a lot of time to explore different lives."

"Different lives? From what John said when I first met him, you were doing the same sort of thing even a hundred years ago."

Another pocket of turbulence shook the plane, and neither spoke until the flight settled once more.

The corners of Daisy's mouth turned up again. "Despite your assumption, I haven't done the same thing throughout my life. I rotate through the decades and have followed many different paths. You must understand how things were before the truth of Oriceran emerged. Travel between the worlds was heavily restricted. Open magic was also severely prohibited, but if you were already over here and could keep a low profile, you had many opportunities. The other thing you have to understand is that humans are all short-lived, so everyone's similar. They all scramble to make a difference before they die, so they tend to do the same thing instead of exploring options."

"I think every living being is like that on some level."

Daisy shook her head. "When you live a lot longer, there is less pressure. Life becomes slower, in a sense, and more sedate—at least it is for many long-lived people." She smiled deprecatingly. "I've always been different."

"Different?"

She nodded. "Think of it as elf ADHD. I'm restless and always feel like I might miss out on something. So, every couple of decades, I mix it up. I change my life and my identity. Often, also my name."

"Is that why you agreed to help me?"

"That's one of the reasons."

The plane entered another turbulent zone, and she frowned. Daniel respected her focus, and his lingering questions remained unasked. He'd run into the beautiful elf on and off for years, but until that moment, he had never realized how little he knew about her.

It'll be interesting to get to know you, Daisy. Very interesting.

Daisy glanced down at her instruments. "We should reach the coordinates any second now."

"It looks like more desert to me." Daniel frowned.

"What did you expect? A giant crashed alien spaceship?" The elf chuckled quietly.

Daniel snorted. "We found piles of bodies in the middle of nowhere before, so at this point, a crashed alien space-ship wouldn't surprise me."

"I'll give you that. I—"

The engine cut out, along with every light and display in the cockpit. Violent tremors shook the plane, and Daisy's fingers turned white as she gripped the yoke. She yanked it back and flipped several switches.

Daniel's heart rate kicked up and his stomach tightened. He bit back his instinctive comments, because the last thing Daisy needed was the distraction of a non-pilot.

She gritted her teeth and kept up her tension on the control yoke, but the desert closed in fast. "Damned piece of junk." She shook her head. "We've lost all power, including to the flaps and the engine. We're going down."

Daniel nodded grimly. "EMP?"

"Maybe." Daisy drew a ragged breath. "We don't have enough glide on this plane. It's now a metal potato."

"So, this is how we go out?" Daniel laughed despite his pounding heart. "At least it's fucking dramatic."

She narrowed her eyes. "Screw that. I still have a few more careers I need to explore." She nodded to the co-pilot yoke. "Grab that."

"I don't know shit about flying planes."

"Just grab it." Daisy winced. "The impact will shred this

plane. There's no way we'll survive unless I do something and that something requires you to grab that."

"You have an idea?" He glanced over his shoulder. "Parachutes?"

"Not enough time. Hold that tight and pull back gently to bring the nose up a little. Keep us as steady as you can. I'll try to throw up a shield spell at the last moment to absorb the impact. We should survive. Maybe." She shrugged. "Hopefully."

Daniel laughed. "More than a zero chance of survival is still better than none." He grabbed the co-pilot yoke, gripped it tightly, and eased it back.

Daisy threw her arms up. Glowing arcane glyphs illuminated the leather bomber jacket she wore over her catsuit. Despite the situation, Daniel couldn't help but wonder at the fact that magical symbols always appeared on her arms no matter what she wore. Did she always wear magic clothing or did it mean something else entirely?

Yeah. There's still so much I don't know about her. If we make it out of this, maybe I should change that sooner rather than later.

The ground hurtled toward them. The secondary mechanical altimeter continued to spin down.

One thousand feet. Nine hundred. Eight hundred.

The glyphs on Daisy's arms brightened, and a shimmering skin of light wrapped around the airplane. She hissed and grimaced.

Five hundred feet. Four hundred.

The elf opened her mouth and a beautiful polyphonic melody emerged. Daniel had never heard her speak in her untranslated native language. The light around the plane intensified to almost unbearable brightness.

Two hundred feet. One hundred. Fifty.

The jet slammed into the ground and tilted as it bounced. A wing gouged into the ground and sheared off with the force of impact. Daisy's breathing became ragged.

Daniel's stomach lurched as the plane flipped and landed again, not bouncing this time. The blinding light from the spell forced his eyes closed. Tearing metal screamed all around them. His safety belt pinned him in his seat as the contents of his stomach sloshed.

Silence finally descended, and both Daniel and Daisy heaved deep sighs of relief.

The agent groaned and shook his head. It felt as heavy as his body. He opened his eyes and blinked. The magical light was gone, and the harsh Australian sun blazed down on him. The rear half of the plane lay in the distance, and pieces of their equipment formed a scattered line of debris. After a few seconds, he realized he was upside-down. All the pouches in his tactical vest remained closed, and both his guns were still tucked in their holsters.

Huh. Next time I fly, I'd better make sure I carry all my gear on me. At least I still have weapons and ammo with me.

He turned to look at Daisy. She was pale and drew shallow breaths, her eyes closed. The glyphs had vanished.

"Are you okay, Daisy? You still with me?"

The elf nodded quickly, and her eyes fluttered open. "That spell...took a lot out of me."

Daniel unfastened his safety belt and grunted as he fell onto the roof of the plane. "Better tired than dead." He reached up and unfastened her belt. She dropped into his arms, and her hot breath heated his face. If his heart hadn't already been racing, it might have gone into high gear.

Daisy blinked, pushed out of his arms, and backed away. "It's like they say, any landing you can walk away from is a good one."

The agent stepped out of the plane and shielded his face against the glare. "It looks like most of our stuff is gone." He retrieved his phone, and the display lit up. "Maybe it wasn't an EMP. It didn't kill the phone." With a few commands, he switched the device to satellite mode. "And I get satellite signal, so there's no general anti-electrical field around here either."

Daisy checked her device and nodded. "Mine's still working, too." She tapped it a few times. "And, yeah, the satellite link is good."

"At least we can call for extraction. We might as well explore the site since we're not dead." Daniel peered at his phone. "According to the GPS, we're a few miles away from the coordinates."

A warm wind blew across his face. The red sand stretched for miles in every direction. The entire area was dotted with shrubs, pointy spinifex grass, and the occasional scrawny tree. Two tall mesas stood in the general area of the coordinates.

Daniel patted his pocket. "I'm glad I had Nessie's sensor wand on me instead of in our unfortunate luggage. She said this latest model is even more sensitive and easy to use."

Daisy looked at the sky and removed her jacket. "Well, it's hot, but it could be worse. I think I'll leave my jacket here."

"We probably won't come back to the wreckage." Daniel rubbed the back of his neck. "Tim will need to pull a few strings and get ASIS out here to clean it up. Maybe they can retrieve your jacket."

She waved a hand dismissively. "I have a lot of them. It's not like it's magic or anything."

Daniel nodded, filing that detail away for the future.

The elf frowned and glanced over her shoulder.

"What's wrong?"

She shook her head. "It's probably nothing, but I felt I was being watched for a moment."

Daniel studied their surroundings. A falcon flew overhead, but that was the only sign of life. "Magic?"

"I don't feel any."

"We both just survived a plane crash, so perhaps our instincts are a little haywire." The agent shrugged. "We should probably head to the coordinates."

Daisy nodded, but her slight frown didn't ease. "Sure."

They set off with the satellite GPS guiding them. Daniel checked over his shoulder a few times but saw nothing more suspicious than animals. Too many questions weighed on him. The plane's total electrical failure could not be an accident, for one thing. The timing was too convenient.

"Did you sense any magic when the plane went down?" the agent asked.

"No."

"Then it was an EMP powerful enough to take down a jet but not affect our phones. That's incredibly specific target capability or a different type of technology." He scowled at the thought.

"What are you getting at?"

He squinted as he focused on the two mesas. "Let's say I wouldn't be surprised to find a few aliens waiting for us at our destination."

Daniel wiped sweat from his brow as they approached the coordinates. No aliens waited for them, at least none he could see. The two mesas formed a natural canyon, the deep basin between them filled with the same sand, plants, and occasional lizards or rodents they'd seen as they trekked the few miles to the site. Nothing seemed unusual or dangerous, and they hadn't even seen a sinister-looking snake or two.

"Huh," the agent mumbled. "I expected a hotter reception."

"Better nothing than a drop bear or a bunyip." Daisy shrugged and looked around. "Ever run into a bunyip?"

He shook his head. "I haven't had the pleasure. The Company doesn't usually send me to fight Australian monsters in the middle of nowhere." He removed the sensor wand and interfaced it with his phone for better data recording. Nessie's preprogramming made the initial scan effortless.

"Did you find anything interesting?" Daisy asked.

Daniel nodded. "Yes. The energy signatures are consistent with what we saw in Baja California and what you found in China."

"It's definitely an alien site, then."

He studied a few graphs on his phone. "Yes, but there are no bodies here."

"There weren't in China, either. They might be previously used sites." Daisy shrugged.

"Yeah." The agent walked toward the mesas. "If I had to guess, I'd say the energy signature is residue from the alien's portal technology. They've probably been here at some point, but who knows when? It could have been last week, or it could have been fifty years ago. The thing I still don't understand is why the plane went down."

Daisy's eyes widened and she drew her pistol. Her glyphs glowed brightly on her arms, and she winced in pain. "Damn it. I'm still strained from the crash, so I won't be one hundred percent with magic."

"What do you see?" Daniel swiveled his head, looking for a target.

"It's not what I see. It's what I feel." Daisy gritted her teeth. "There was no magic at all, and suddenly, there was a massive amount."

"But wh—"

Four bright pinpoints of light appeared. They expanded into four swirling portals and surrounded the team. The bright light forced Daniel to blink and shield his eyes.

The agent yanked out a silver handgun with a narrow barrel and only the tiniest hole in the front—Nessie's advanced blast pistol. Daisy aimed her more conventional 9mm at one of the portals.

Daisy and Daniel stood back to back, both poised and waiting for an enemy to appear.

Naked men and women with rotting flesh stumbled from the portals. Skeletons joined them. It was an army of the damned, mere flesh and bone weaponized and programmed to kill.

"Necromancy," Daniel grunted. "Do you have any idea how to shoot a skeleton to death?"

Daisy snorted. "They're already dead."

"With zombies, you take the head out, right?"

"It doesn't always work, but massive amounts of physical damage can disrupt the spells animating the bodies or skeletons." Daisy sighed. "There's only so much I can do. I haven't had enough time to recover, and my magic tends to focus more on personal enhancement."

"We'll figure something out." Daniel laughed. "I guess I shouldn't feel bitter about not having sonic grenades and be glad Nessie let me bring the nice gun. Fortunately, I didn't lose it in the crash."

The undead still issued from the portals, but they didn't advance. Instead, they formed a circle of dead warriors and stared at the pair with their empty eye sockets. After a few moments, the stream of monsters ceased, but dozens of enemies now surrounded them.

Neither the agent nor the elf fired. No immediate attack meant they might still find a way through the horde.

Three of the portals vanished, and a tall woman in a red dress stepped through the fourth. She was slender and attractive, though her face was too angular and severe for Daniel to call her beautiful. Her long fingers gripped a dark wand tipped with bone. The gateway closed behind her.

The agent exhaled sharply. "A random necromancer witch I don't recognize. You must be Morgana."

Her smile was icy and her gaze flicked to Daisy for a moment before it focused on him. "I heard you finally got my message and wanted to meet me. I decided to indulge your whim."

She spoke with a faint accent, but he couldn't place it.

The elf snorted in disdain.

"So you took my plane down to get me here?" Daniel responded with a shrug and aimed his weapon calmly at Morgana. "Well, now I'm here."

She laughed. "Your plane? I had nothing to do with that. I didn't even know you were on a plane."

Daniel frowned. The witch had no reason to lie at this point, but it didn't make sense. "I conveniently crashed, and then you show up?"

"Convenience had nothing to do with it. I've waited for an opportunity." She glared at his partner. "I didn't realize you had an elf helping you. I thought your kind didn't rely on magicals except temporarily. She made things…more complicated, but when her suppression spell weakened, I had an opportunity."

"Sorry for the inconvenience, you crazy necromancer bitch," Daisy muttered.

"Don't worry, little elf. I'll enjoy experimenting on your body after I'm done with Daniel."

The CIA agent chuckled. "I don't even know who you are, other than a necromancer who has it in for me. What, did you pick my name from a hat and decide to fuck with me?"

Morgana chuckled quietly, but there was no mirth in the sound. "I suppose it can't be helped that you don't recognize me, even if you did kill me once."

"You look good for a dead woman." Daniel blew out a breath to release a little of the tension he felt. "I suppose all that organ-harvesting was to help your necromancy? Do you need organs when you body-hop?"

She sneered. "I'm disappointed, but I suppose I should have expected such disrespect. I almost thought you would recognize me from my bearing, but it's no matter. I'm happy to pay you a visit, Daniel, and I couldn't have asked for you to isolate yourself better."

"You're insane. How many people have you killed?"

Morgana barked out a laugh. "How many have *you*?"

Daniel narrowed his eyes. "I don't go to villages and murder innocent people. I don't rip their organs from their bodies for my insane magical experiments." He shook his head. "Sure, I have blood on my hands, but your body is drenched in it. So spare me the lecture, you twisted, crazy monster."

Daisy frowned. "I sense more magic."

He twitched his finger, but Morgana hadn't raised her wand.

Another swirling portal appeared. Julia stepped out, a smirk on her face and her hands behind her back. The gate shimmered and vanished.

"I know how you found me now," Daniel mumbled.

The elf rolled her eyes. "I knew the spell was a bad idea."

CHAPTER NINETEEN

The agent shook his head and aimed his gun at Julia. "It made an effective sob story. I can usually see through that kind of thing, but you played your part well."

Julia brought her hand forward, her white wand at the ready. "I should have killed you in London."

"I'm hard to kill. Kind of like a cockroach that way." Daniel glanced at Morgana. "Apparently, so are you."

The glyphs brightened on Daisy's arms but she held her gun up. "You'll need a pile of new bodies to hop into by the time we're done with you."

"Such idle threats, but I don't even need to kill you." Morgana slashed through the air with her wand and flicked it. "I'll enjoy seeing them tear you apart. Goodbye, Daniel. Better luck in your next life."

The zombies and skeletons advanced in short, plodding steps. Daisy motioned quickly with her hands, and a bright aura surrounded both her and Daniel. The elf hissed in pain.

Julia laughed. "Did that tiny amount of magic strain you? Pathetic elf."

"I don't suppose you know how to turn undead, do you, Daisy?" Daniel asked.

She blinked. "Huh? Turn undead?"

"It's a long story. Don't worry about it."

Daisy fired. Julia stumbled back and blood sprayed from her wound, but she smiled and straightened.

"You thought that would be enough?" She chuckled and shook her head. Her wounds began to knit closed. "I told you in London that we use life magic, and I further specialize in regeneration."

Daniel aimed at the woman and pulled the trigger. A blue beam shot from his blast pistol, accompanied by a faint buzz. The witch screamed as the energy burned a hole through her chest. She collapsed to her knees. Two shots to her head and two more to her chest left a headless and heartless corpse. The seared wounds didn't mend.

"Regenerate from *that*," he taunted.

Morgana pursed her lips and shook her head. She clutched her wand in front of her. "Pathetic."

Daisy smirked, although sweat trailed down her face. "It's hard to get good lackeys these days, huh?" She nodded to Daniel. "Your gun is bigger than mine in this case."

"I'd hope so." He fired at Morgana, but the beam crashed into an invisible barrier and dissipated.

She wagged her finger. "Are you afraid yet?"

He nodded at Julia. "You're the person with a dead friend."

"A tool, not a friend."

The agent fired again, and Daisy joined him. Neither beam nor bullet reached the witch. She fake-yawned and patted her mouth. The horde was barely yards away from the pair now.

"Fuck," he muttered. The agent spun and blew a zombie's head off, but the body continued to advance. He shot it through the heart, and the corpse toppled backward and lay still. His follow-up attempt with a skeleton left a headless body closing in on him. A shot through a leg reduced it to a crawling decapitated skeleton.

Daisy tried eliminating a zombie with a headshot followed by another to its heart, but it barely slowed. All she accomplished with a skeleton was to add a new skull hole. The bones moved forward relentlessly, the pointed, fleshless fingers ready to rend them apart. Daniel vaporized another zombie's head and chest, his frown now fixed in place.

This is not how I thought today would unfold.

The indicator on the back of the blast pistol flashed red. His power cell was almost drained.

"This thing's better for assassination than real fights," he muttered.

"I still don't know who you are," Daniel yelled, "so killing me now won't accomplish what you want."

"What I *want*?" Morgana replied. "What I want is for you to die, Daniel Winters."

Daisy leaned toward him and whispered, "I can maybe clear a path, but not much more. Most of my spells enhance me rather than blow things up. The shields I put around us won't last long."

"You're strained to the limit already, so I don't think

that's a good idea." He managed to destroy another skeleton.

A loud crackle sounded behind them, and a pulsing green orb slammed into a zombie and disintegrated the top half. Two more shots obliterated another zombie and the upper half of a skeleton. The bones stopped moving.

The two spun toward the source of the shots.

Jake held a squat, metallic black-and-red pistol with a twisting barrel. He fired a green orb of death to demolish another of Morgana's horde.

Daniel stared at the alien for a moment, unsure how to react before turning toward the witch. "Daisy, do you have enough juice left to give me one shot?"

The elf glanced at Jake. "What about him?"

"Let's worry about the woman trying to kill us right now."

Daisy holstered her pistol and raised her arms. "It's a tragedy when a long life comes to an end. Make sure mine doesn't, Daniel."

The glyphs on her arm intensified, and the shields vanished. She gritted her teeth and held her hands close together. Strands of light gathered to form a glowing ball between her palms.

The alien annihilated several more zombies and skeletons. His weapon might not have the horrific power of a transformation gun, but Daniel's blast pistol was a pathetic squirt gun in comparison.

Morgana's face twitched, and she backed away. She held her wand with both hands, her brow lowered as she glared at him.

Daisy's orb continued to build. "What's the matter,

witch? Does it take all your concentration and power to keep your toys up and running? Maybe you should have taken us on without them."

The elf thrust her arms out, and her white orb rocketed forward. The blinding ball of white light crashed into Morgana's invisible barrier and exploded in a shower of white sparks.

The witch cried out and stumbled back.

"Do it, Daniel!" Daisy yelled. "The shield is down." She fell to her hands and knees and dragged in deep breaths.

The agent fired the blast pistol. The blue beam blew a hole through Morgana's chest, and she crumpled to her knees, her eyes wide in shock. He smirked and pulled the trigger again. The weapon beeped and didn't fire.

The indicator light glowed solid red. He was out of power.

The alien aimed toward the necromancer and fired, but a zombie caught the blast instead.

Daniel dropped the blast pistol and yanked his handgun free to fire several rounds into the kneeling Queen of Hearts. She jerked with each slug, and her blood mingled with the scarlet fabric of her dress. Two more shots struck her in the head, and she slumped backward.

Morgana groaned, her eyes closed, and flourished her wand. A swirling portal opened beneath her, and she dropped into it as Daniel and Daisy both fired. The gateway vanished.

The remaining zombies and skeletons crumpled to the ground and lay motionless, but Jake had already carved through half the horde with his alien weapon.

The agent exhaled on a curse. "All the strings cut at once, huh?"

Daisy frowned and stared at the alien. "I don't know if this is over."

Daniel looked at the counterfeit boy who now had his weapon trained on them.

He tossed his gun to the ground and raised his hands. "I suppose that even if I tried to shoot you, you have some ridiculously advanced alien shield to bounce my beam clean off."

"Does it work against magic?" Daisy pushed herself up and flexed her hands. Dim glyphs lit her arms.

Jake snorted. "Try what you want, elf. See if you can do it before I kill you both."

She glanced at her partner, and he shook his head. The glyphs disappeared when she lowered her arms.

Daniel shrugged. "If you wanted to kill me, it would have made sense to simply let Morgana do it."

"If I had wanted to kill you, I didn't need to follow you to Australia to do it." Jake shrugged but kept the weapon aimed unwaveringly at Daniel.

The CIA agent furrowed his brow. "Did you take out the plane?"

The alien snorted. "No. You came here for a reason. Well, now that you know some places are…touched, it shouldn't be a surprise that some can cause interesting problems. I'm amazed you didn't die, though."

"What do you want?" Daniel asked. "It's been a pretty sucky day. I'd like to get it over with one way or another."

Jake gestured with the gun. "You know what I want. The control rod."

"Come on. You've obviously followed me around and observed me. Do you still think I have the damned thing?" He shrugged and scrubbed a hand over his face. "It's long gone, taken by a powerful elf who wanted to make sure that stupid humans like myself couldn't use the damned gun."

Jake blinked several times, obvious shock on his face. "You expect me to believe such a pathetic lie?"

Daniel laughed. "I'm CIA. If I lied, it wouldn't be pathetic. No. Do you want the truth? The elf told my grandfather about the gun, and he sent me after it. I acquired it and stuck it in a vault. Then my grandfather removed the rod, copied it, and gave the real one to a powerful magical who would never have a reason to use the gun. That's the sad thing about all this. Everyone has lied about your damned fucking gun because anyone who sees it realizes that it's too dangerous to use."

Daisy crossed her arms and watched in silence, her brow knitted.

"You mentioned a trade," Jake replied. "Back in Alexandria."

"Because I was stalling you." Daniel face-palmed. "It's gone. *I'll* never see it again, and *you* won't ever see it again. If you don't believe me, run an alien lie detector over me." He waved a hand dismissively. "You'd know better than I would, but the gun has all the dangerous parts, right? And you have the gun. The rod's useless tech without it. Sure, someone might reverse-engineer it, but without the actual weapon, what would that accomplish?"

Jake's gun wavered, and his arm dropped. He sighed. "I don't need a device to know you're telling the truth, Agent

Winters. I'd convinced myself that you would lead me to it, but I think I always knew what I'd find."

Daniel closed his eyes and blew out a breath. "Then what's your real game?"

Daisy shot him a warning glance, but he shook his head at her.

"My game?" Jake replied.

"Yes. You come to our planet and kidnap people. I don't understand. Half the time I think you're ruthless spies preparing for an invasion, but the rest of the time I'm not sure. I don't doubt that you could have taken and tortured me for information with devices I can't even begin to imagine instead of following me around."

The alien snorted. "Typical human. The first thing you think of is violence. Your species is barbaric, backward, and cruel."

Daisy frowned. "And what about elves? You had an elf you exchanged for prisoners. Are you coming to Oriceran, too?"

"Our…excursions are limited to Earth. He happened to be here." Jake scoffed. "That's what he gets for being around barbarians."

"I'm not the one with a gun that can twist a man into a pretzel." Daniel pointed angrily at his adversary. "Why the hell are you on Earth? If you don't want to bumble into a war with Earth or Oriceran, then you need to use the fucking front door, not skulk in the back armed to the teeth."

Something subtle played across Jake's face, and some of the hostility drifted away. "We have our reasons, but it's not my decision to share those with you."

The CIA agent stomped forward. Jake's hand twitched, but he didn't raise the gun.

I'm tired of this bullshit, especially when I'm so close.

"You people have my parents, don't you?" Daniel shouted. "Where the hell are they?"

Daisy sighed. "Daniel, calm down."

"No. I won't. If he wants to kill me, he can go ahead and do it, but like you wouldn't stop looking for the control rods, Jake, I won't give up on my parents." The agent curled his hands into fists. "I don't give a shit what your secret plan is. If you're here to harm Earth or Oriceran I'll stop you, even if you're not doing it intentionally. If you're here in peace, then fucking *prove* it and tell me where my damned parents are."

Jake stared at him. The seconds ticked by while the alien and the human locked eyes, their faces tight.

"You aren't ready for the truth," Jake muttered.

Daniel snorted. "Think what you want, but I meant what I said. The only way to stop me is to kill me." He gestured toward the dead Julia and the collapsed undead army. "And as you can see, you'll have to get in line."

The alien smirked and retrieved a metallic silver-green rod-shaped device with grooves. Daniel recognized the communicator immediately. The pseudo-boy pressed into the grooves, and it came to life. His fingers made a few quick motions over it.

"Things are different here," he said finally, his voice a near-whisper.

Daniel glared at him. "What's that supposed to mean?"

"There's more potential in this place," Jake admitted. "You'll see soon enough."

A massive shadow enveloped not only the boy but most of the area as well. Everything shimmered for a moment, except for the small islands of untouched and reddened sand beneath Daisy and Daniel's feet. The region darkened, the harsh light of the Outback sun all but non-existent.

The elf sucked in a breath and her partner narrowed his eyes.

Is this it? Are the aliens finally done with me?

Shadowy humanoid forms appeared, followed by the outlines of densely-packed buildings in a variety of designs —some thin and angular, others rounded with flat or curved roofs. The vista resembled an insane architect's playground. Trees lined pathways and roads, but there were no vehicles.

The tenebrous forms grew denser in a holographic display with only shades of gray and black. Dozens of people walked around, perhaps hundreds. The trees swayed, touched by an unknown wind. He couldn't tell the species with the lack of detail and the distance, but they didn't look different from anything he'd seen on his Earth travels.

"Is that why you came here?" Daniel muttered. "Because our planet is similar to yours? Do you claim to be refugees?"

"I claim nothing," Jake replied. "I'm showing you." He became a living shadow, and the blackness swallowed him piecemeal.

Daniel grunted. He was tired of being toyed with. The aliens might be advanced, but he refused to take their shit. He looked up, and his eyes widened.

Impossible.

The dark forms of a man and woman appeared. He saw more wrinkles and different hairstyles, and some details were obscured in the darkness, but there was no way he wouldn't recognize them.

Daniel reached out. "Mom, Dad…"

The massive pool of darkness vanished, the entire area brightened, and Daniel stared between the two massive mesas, doubting his own eyes.

"Daisy," he whispered.

"Yes, Daniel?"

He exhaled a little of the pain that shafted through his heart. "Did you see some sort of city with people?"

The elf nodded cautiously. "Yes."

"I'm sure I saw my parents, but they looked older." His voice remained almost a whisper. "I don't understand. Kevin, Yarvin, and Chen hadn't aged, but the bodies we found at the Baja site obviously had. It looks like my parents have, too."

Daisy sighed. "Clones?"

"Maybe, but there was something about the expressions on their faces. I doubt it."

She shrugged. "I'm sure there are answers to those questions, but we won't find them in the middle of the desert. Besides, you now know the answer to the most important question."

Daniel frowned and looked her way. "And what's that?"

"Your parents are alive." Daisy fumbled for her phone. "It's time to call for extraction."

Daniel allowed himself a feral grin as he stepped into Lucky's. He'd thought about this moment since his return from Australia. Revenge wasn't always necessary but implied revenge was good policy in his dangerous line of work.

His survey of the bar netted him his target, a man in a gaudy purple velvet suit nestled in the darkness of a poorly lit corner.

Daniel marched toward the table, weaving to avoid staggering patrons and waitresses with trays filled with drinks and food. Ralph looked up, his face tight and his lips pursed. He didn't run, but that could indicate either bravery or arrogance—not that it mattered.

The CIA agent grinned and dropped into the chair across from his quarry. "It's almost like you're surprised to see me."

The man rubbed the back of his neck. "Nah. It's been one of those days, that's all."

Daniel leaned forward. "Do you know why you're still breathing, Ralph?"

"I have no idea what you mean."

"Rule #1, Ralph. That's the only reason. I should kill you since you led me right into a trap."

The informant winced and held his palms out. "I'm simply an information broker. I occasionally get a bum tip. I'm sorry."

Daniel snorted. "Words, Ralph. They mean nothing." He stood and straightened his lapels and his tie with steady movements. "Keep in mind that Lucky's rules only apply here, and you don't live here."

Ralph swallowed. "Come on, man. I'm sure I can make it up to you."

"Oh yes, you will. You'll make it right." The agent leaned one arm on the table and glared at Ralph. "Or you'd better beg Lucky to let you sleep here twenty-four-seven." He straightened and plastered a smile on his face. "Now, I'll head to the bar and order a drink. I must follow the rules, after all. Maybe I'll even ask to listen to some Pavarotti. But here's some advice, Ralph. Don't be here when I'm done with that drink. Sure, we all make mistakes, and I might make one once I have some IPA in me."

With that, he sauntered to the bar and didn't bother to look over his shoulder.

Aliens and necromancers and betrayal. They're all part of a typical week now.

Tommy sat in a chair, crouched over a table, his attention focused on the comic book in front of him. He looked up after a couple of minutes. Daniel leaned against the wall of the back room of Rooney's Antiquities and Oddities with his arms folded.

"Oh, I didn't even hear you come in, dude."

"That's me. Silent as a cat." Daniel smiled. "I wanted to see if you're fully settled in. I know I've been all over the world on acquisition trips, so I wasn't sure."

The kid blinked. "Why? Did Mr. Rooney say something?"

The agent shook his head. "Not at all, but you let your father leave you home alone with nothing but ramen cups, so you don't seem to know when to complain about your living situation."

Tommy shrugged. "It's not like things are that different. I was basically living here before."

"Sleeping on a cot in a back room isn't the same thing as living upstairs in the apartment."

The half-elf smiled. "Yeah, I guess you're right. It isn't. But you don't have to worry, dude. I'm doing great. I appreciate everything you and Mr. Rooney are doing for me."

Daniel adopted a serious expression. "I know you understand that while you're under our roof, you follow our rules. I have two I care about, one I came up with and one Pops suggested."

"Okay, sure." Tommy shrugged. "Bring it on."

The agent held up a single finger. "First, you go to school unless you're sick. There's no way you will ever study robotics without a proper education."

"Sure, sure. That's fair."

He held up another finger and grinned playfully. "Second, you need to earn your keep."

Tommy nodded. "Like chores and stuff?"

"Pops had a better idea. I'm supposed to run this shop, but I'm so busy on my acquisitions trips that it doesn't always work out that way. We want you to work part-time in the shop. Paid, of course."

The boy's eyes widened. "Woah, dude. I've never had a job before." He laughed. "A half-elf working in a magic item shop. It's like on Oriceran."

Daniel smiled. Sometimes the smallest victories were the most satisfying.

The agent waved to Tommy as the boy headed off to school. The thump of feet on the stairs caught his attention. His grandfather stopped at the bottom and watched the kid disappear down the street.

Peter nodded toward the counter. "Put your toy down."

"Sure." Daniel retrieved the silence cube from his pocket and activated it. "This isn't something you normally worry about."

"Maybe it's time I was more careful." Peter shrugged. "You've picked up a lot of enemies in the world, Daniel, between necromancers and aliens. I wish I could trace Underwood and get the rod back, but he's not the kind of guy you look up on the internet."

"It's not important." The agent shook his head. "Jake might not be my friend, but I don't think he's my enemy."

The old man sighed. "He did save you, even if it was for his own reasons, but that must mean something."

"It goes beyond that," Daniel replied. "This is the second time I've been in a remote area with aliens with advanced technology. The gun he used wasn't as terrifying as the Munich gun and its brother, but it could easily have killed Daisy and me."

Peter grunted. "It's not like you kill people if you don't have a reason to, so why should the aliens?"

"Exactly." Daniel walked to a nearby shelf and stared at a white-and-red *maneki neko.* The arm of the Japanese beckoning cat statue moved as his gaze settled on it. He looked away, and the cat stopped moving. "I don't trust them. They have Mom and Dad, but I think they are far less dangerous than Fortis believes."

His grandfather scowled. "Maybe your parents have a reason to be there. The important thing is that they're alive." He drew a shaky breath. They might be Daniel's parents, but they were Peter's son-in-law and daughter too.

"Maybe, but I can't know why if the damned aliens won't tell me." Daniel frowned. "And every time we move forward, something kicks us back. The locational database failed the other day, then the communications device went dead. Ronni and Big Gnome think the aliens somehow killed them remotely. It's possible they knew we had them and simply strung us along while Jake looked for the guns. Or, hell, maybe the gadgets simply ran out of power. We thought we were reverse engineering them but were merely discovering how to use them, which isn't the same thing at all."

"You still have the devices. I'm sure they will learn something more."

Daniel shrugged. "I don't know. Imagine if a smartphone turned up in the Middle Ages. A peasant could figure out how to access the programs and menus if it wasn't locked, but the minute the power ran out, they'd be stymied. Even if you gave an educated aristocrat a book that explained the principles of the electronics involved, they couldn't produce what was necessary to recharge the device."

Peter folded his arms. "What's your plan, then?"

"The same as before. We investigate alien activity and continue to seek other technology." Daniel exhaled a frustrated sigh. "The CIA has no more prisoners at headquarters, and I don't know if they recaptured any aliens. We need to convince the damned aliens to talk and actually explain some crap." He nodded to a globe sitting atop a shelf. "If they aren't invaders, what are they doing here? There are still so many things I don't understand like that dead woman and the alien cloning her body. Did they have a reason to kill her?" He shrugged helplessly. "For all I know, she was a secret Fortis agent and it was self-defense, but that doesn't explain why they've taken people and to where. I didn't see anything that looked like the interior of a ship. It appeared to be a planet similar to ours. They can teleport people over vast distances in a way that even Oricerans can't accomplish."

His grandfather smiled. "You've already seen and learned a lot more than we ever did in my Army unit. You know what I always said back in the day whenever one of the new guys got frustrated?"

"What?"

"If you've got a question, keep pushing until you find the answer or you drop dead." Peter grinned.

Daniel chuckled and nodded. "I'll do that, Pops." He stepped to the globe and spun it. "And wherever they are, I will find my parents."

The End

The past catches up with Daniel in his next adventure, Artifact of the Guardians.

Solve a murder, save her mother, and stop the apocalypse?

No problem.

She has a foul-mouthed troll on her side.

For Austin homicide detective Leira Berens happy is running down bad guys and solving crimes.

And she's damn good at it.

Which is why when the Light Elf prince is murdered, the king breaks a centuries old treaty and crosses between worlds to seek her help.

Wait a minute. An Elf? Like from Lord of the Rings or something?

Yeah, Leira has a hard time accepting that.

But it doesn't matter what she believes.

Magic is real, and it's coming back with a literal bang.

The prince's death was only the beginning. Tracking down his killer is about more than just justice.

It's saving the world.

If you're looking for a heroine who prefers chasing bad guys rather than boyfriends, this book is for you.

AVAILABLE ON AMAZON RETAILERS AND IN KINDLE UNLIMITED

Last Wednesday, my oldest sister, Diana died. I called her D. She was my first hero and everything about her inspired me to always believe my dreams should come true, and that my definition of myself was the only one that mattered. What others think of me is none of my business. Just keep going.

She was ten years older than I am, just old enough that when I was small, I was often watching her to see what was possible. It was the 1960's and she was fearless, already determined as a teenager to be not only a doctor, but a surgeon. I already knew I wanted to be a journalist and an author and tell stories but was painfully aware that the doors wouldn't exactly be flying open for me. But hey, if my big sister could do it, why not me?

She could embroider and cook exotic food from scratch and had deep red hair and loved sci fi and mysteries and had a curiosity about life that was boundless. She also got my share of the math skills and took to it like it was a form of art. A guy once gave her a handmade, large wooden box with a padlock for Christmas. Taped to it was a math puzzle written like a poem. Figure it out, get the combination, get the prize inside.

He thought it would take her hours. Within fifteen minutes she had it open and was holding the jewelry box with the expensive earrings, a triumphant look on her face.

Diana also had a laugh that made you feel like you were in on a joke with her. When my son, who's now 30, liked to play Houdini at the age of three and escape the house, I had to start deadbolting the doors. One night, he took a look at all the people in the kitchen and picked out this particular aunt. "I'll bet you know where the key is."

She laughed, and said conspiratorially, "Wouldn't you like to know." Her laugh had the same effect on him that it had on anyone else. He laughed and fell into her arms, still wondering how to get that key.

And she was too young to have her story end just yet, but that happens. Thing is, Diana would want me to ask, what now? What's the next adventure? Get going, go find out, and along the way, don't forget who you are and don't let others define it for you. Don't take anything too seriously but care about what you're doing and soak up every bit of it while it's happening.

I'm still her little sister and still following right behind her. I'm off to the next adventure and in 2019 I'm going to get out more and meet the fans – ROAD TRIP! – and spend time with the people that I love, enjoy this house, run a 5k or two, get back on my bike, draw more cartoons, dance a helluva lot more, cook a few exotic dishes, write a few good stories with magic inside of them and soak up every bit of it while it's happening. That's the best way I know to keep her story going.

I'm looking forward to seeing what each of us is doing to build a better life and to do it in community. Write to me with your adventures and help me keep the story going. More adventures to follow.

THANK YOU for not only reading this story but these *Author Notes* as well .

(I think I've been good with always opening with "thank you." If not, I need to edit the other *Author Notes*!)

RANDOM (*sometimes*) THOUGHTS?

I spoke about the Stryper concern back in book one, and I thought I might update you folks how that went.

Work for you?

So, the Whiskey A Go-Go is a small venue. There is the main floor – standing room only, and six booths on the far side (to the left as you enter) that you "rent" by agreeing to spend a minimum amount on drink and food.

As a successful author (read, old as shit and not willing to stand for four hours), I was able to grab one of the tinier booths (seats three, we were only two) and I told the waitress if she kept me supplied with Coke (the drink, not the white drug) I would double my tip.

I was damned near sloshing anytime I stood up by the

end of the night, I'd drunk so much Coke I'd had to hit the men's room twice already.

(Oh, there is a half-sized second-floor area where you could drink and watch as well. We went up there for the band's signing event, which was cool.)

The funny event of the evening was when a prim and proper (at least) fifty-five-year-old man grabbed the booth next to us.

It had a $200.00 minimum. He was very dapper (I'd say he was dressed spiffy and it looked like the suit style was from at least forty years ago. Not that the suit was that old, but it had an air of class you don't normally see.

His booth could have easily fit nine.

During the concerts (there were many), people came by, and at one time an attractive young woman asked to sit with my younger brother and me.

He's in a relationship, I'm married to a Hispanic woman.

Sorry, but No *F'ing Way* was she getting to sit in that tiny area! I turned to the guy next to us and suggested, "He has room!"

She went to ask him, he was HAPPY to have her sit with him, and they left the concert before the final band got on stage. His hand was on her back.

There was at least thirty-five years difference between them.

Now, I'm not the best judge of people, but I personally believe both of them were (in some way) con artists. I'm not suggesting I know what they were each selling, but it looked like she was selling a physically good time (in exchange for something besides cash), and he was selling "Hollywood."

If that is true, they deserved each other.

Oh, as a side note, the concert was fantastic!

HOW TO MARKET FOR BOOKS YOU LOVE

We are able to support our efforts with you reading our books, and we appreciate you doing this!

If you enjoyed this or ANY book by any author, especially Indie-published, we always appreciate if you make the time to review a book, since it lets other readers who might be on the fence to take a chance on it as well.

AROUND THE WORLD IN 80 DAYS

One of the interesting (at least to me) aspects of my life is the ability to work from anywhere and at any time. In the future, I hope to re-read my own *Author Notes* and remember my life as a diary entry.

Right now, I'm sitting at the kitchen table in our La Puente, Ca home. Joseph (youngest child, presently in his sophomore year at University of Texas – Arlington) is playing tunes and working on his homework, this being the Thanksgiving holidays.

He flies back tomorrow, and we head back to Las Vegas Sunday morning.

We had the first official family event here this Thanksgiving, and it was really nice. This house has been in the family for thirty-five-plus years and was recently renovated after a seriously bad experience with renters trashing the place.

Jacob and I tossed out rye seed for the coming winter months.

(When you read "Jacob and I," you should read it as "Jacob, with supervisory effort by his dad.")

Then, the guys (Jacob and Joseph) and I put up a RING video doorbell and (Joseph and I – see note above) put up the RING stick-up video camera.)

Now my damned phone is chiming every time someone goes into the garage because of a reflection issue I didn't think about when installing the motion-detecting camera INSIDE the garage next to a window.

Plus, the video recording is upside down (another failure I need to fix. I didn't think we needed to place it higher until I set up the camera on the phone app.)

So, for RING I'd give it a 9/10 for installation ease (even for the drilling into the brick/stucco exterior) because everything was in the box (including masonry drill bit.)

Quality of video? That's a 6.5/10 at the moment.

FAN PRICING

If you would like to find out what LMBPN is doing and the books we will be publishing, just sign up at http:// lmbpn.com/email/. When you sign up, we notify you of books coming out for the week, any new posts of interest in the books and pop culture arena, and the fan pricing on Saturday.

Ad Aeternitatem,

Michael Anderle

Other series in the Oriceran Universe:
THE DANIEL CODEX SERIES
I FEAR NO EVIL
THE UNBELIEVABLE MR. BROWNSTONE
SCHOOL OF NECESSARY MAGIC
THE LEIRA CHRONICLES
REWRITING JUSTICE
THE KACY CHRONICLES
MIDWEST MAGIC CHRONICLES
SOUL STONE MAGE
THE FAIRHAVEN CHRONICLES

OTHER BOOKS BY JUDITH BERENS

OTHER BOOKS BY MARTHA CARR